D1084595

DOMNEI

DOMNEI

A COMEDY OF WOMAN-WORSHIP
BY JAMES BRANCH CABELL
WITH AN INTRODUCTION BY
JOSEPH HERGESHEIMER • • •

"En cor gentil domnei per mort no passa."

BOOKS FOR LIBRARIES PRESS
FREEPORT, NEW YORK

First Published 1920

Reprinted 1970 by arrangement with
Mrs. James Branch Cabell

INTERNATIONAL STANDARD BOOK NUMBER:
0-8369-5549-8

LIBRARY OF CONGRESS CATALOG CARD NUMBER:
75-133517

PRINTED IN THE UNITED STATES OF AMERICA

TO

SARAH READ McADAMS

IN GRATITUDE AND AFFECTION

"The complication of opinions and ideas, of affections and habits, which prompted the chevalier to devote himself to the service of a lady, and by which he strove to prove to her his love, and to merit hers in return, was expressed, in the language of the Troubadours, by a single word, by the word *domnei*, a derivation of *domna*, which may be regarded as an alteration of the Latin *domina*, lady, mistress."

—C. C. Fauriel,
History of Provençal Poetry.

Contents

A PREFACE

BY

JOSEPH HERGESHEIMER

A Preface

IT would be absorbing to discover the present feminine attitude toward the profoundest compliment ever paid women by the heart and mind of men in league—the worshipping devotion conceived by Plato and elevated to a living faith in mediæval France. Through that renaissance of a sublimated passion *domnei* was regarded as a throne of alabaster by the chosen figures of its service: Melicent, at Bellegarde, waiting for her marriage with King Theodoret, held close an image of Perion made of substance that time was powerless to destroy; and which, in a life of singular violence, where blood hung scarlet before men's eyes like a tapestry, burned in a silver flame untroubled by the fate of her body. It was, to her, a magic that kept her inviolable, perpetually, in spite of marauding fingers, a rose in the blanched perfection of its early flowering.

The clearest possible case for that religion was

that it transmuted the individual subject of its adoration into the deathless splendor of a Madonna unique and yet divisible in a mirage of earthly loveliness. It was heaven come to Aquitaine, to the Courts of Love, in shapes of vivid fragrant beauty, with delectable hair lying gold on white samite worked in borders of blue petals. It chose not abstractions for its faith, but the most desirable of all actual—yes, worldly—incentives: the sister, it might be, of Count Emmerick of Poictesme. And, approaching beatitude not so much through a symbol of agony as by the fragile grace of a woman, raising Melicent to the stars, it fused, more completely than in any other aspiration, the spirit and the flesh.

However, in its contact, its lovers' delight, it was no more than a slow clasping and unclasping of the hands; the spirit and flesh, merged, became spiritual; the height of stars was not a figment. . . . Here, since the conception of *domnei* has so utterly vanished, the break between the ages impassable, the sympathy born of understanding is interrupted. Hardly a woman, to-day, would value a sigh the passion which turned a man steadfastly away that he might be with her forever beyond the parched forest of death. Now such emotion is held strictly to the gains, the accountability, of life's immediate span; women have left their cloudy magnificence for a footing on earth; but—at least in warm graceful youth—their dreams are still of a Perion de la Forêt. These, clear-eyed, they disavow; yet their secret desire, the most Elysian of all hopes, to burn at once with the body and the soul, mocks what they find.

That vision, dominating Mr. Cabell's pages, the record of his revealed idealism, brings specially to *Domnei* a beauty finely escaping the dusty confusion of any present. It is a book laid in a purity, a serenity, of space above the vapors, the bigotry and engendered spite, of dogma and creed. True to yesterday, it will be faithful of to-morrow; for, in the evolution of humanity, not necessarily the turn of a wheel upward, certain qualities have remained at the center, undisturbed. And, of these, none is more fixed than an abstract love.

Different in men than in women, it is, for the former, an instinct, a need, to serve rather than be served: their desire is for a shining image superior, at best, to both lust and maternity. This consciousness, grown so dim that it is scarcely perceptible, yet still alive, is not extinguished with youth, but lingers hopeless of satisfaction through the incongruous years of middle age. There is never a man, gifted to any degree with imagination, but eternally searches for an ultimate loveliness not disappearing in the circle of his embrace—the instinctively Platonic gesture toward the only immortality conceivable in terms of ecstasy.

A truth, now, in very low esteem! With the solidification of society, of property, the bond of family has been tremendously exalted, the mere fact of parenthood declared the last sanctity. Together with this, naturally, the persistent errantry of men, so vulgarly misunderstood, has become only a reprehensible paradox. The entire shelf of James Branch Cabell's books, dedicated to an unquenchable masculine idealism, has, as well, a paradoxical place in an age of material sentimentality. Compared with the novels of the moment, *Domnei* is an isolated, a heroic fragment of a vastly deeper and higher structure. And, of its many aspects, it is not impossible that the highest, rising over even its heavenly vision, is the rare, the simple, fortitude of its statement.

Whatever dissent the philosophy of Perion and Melicent may breed, no one can fail to admire the steady courage with which it is upheld. Aside from its special preoccupation, such independence in the face of ponderable threat, such accepted isolation, has a rare stability in a world treacherous with mental quicksands and evasions. This is a valor not drawn from insensibility, but from the sharpest possible recognition of all the evil and Cyclopean forces in existence, and a deliberate engagement of them on their own ground. Nothing more, in that direction, can be asked of Mr. Cabell, of anyone. While about the story itself, the soul of Melicent, the form and incidental writing, it is no longer necessary to speak.

The pages have the rich sparkle of a past like stained glass called to life: the Confraternity of St. Médard presenting their masque of Hercules; the claret colored walls adorned with gold cinquefoils of Demetrios' court; his pavilion with porticoes of Andalusian copper; Theodoret's capital, Megaris, ruddy with bonfires; the free port of Narenta with its sails spread for the land of pagans; the lichen-incrusted glade in the Forest of Columbiers; gardens with the walks sprinkled with crocus and vermilion and powdered mica . . . all are at once real and bright with unreality, rayed with the splendor of an antiquity built from webs and films of imagined wonder. The past is, at its moment, the present, and that lost is valueless. Distilled by time, only an imperishable romantic conception remains; a vision, where it is significant, animated by the feelings, the men and women, which only, at heart, are changeless.

They, the surcharged figures of *Domnei,* move vividly through their stone galleries and closes, in procession, and—a far more difficult accomplishment—alone. The lute of the Bishop of Montors, playing as he rides in scarlet, sounds its Provençal refrain; the old man Theodoret, a king, sits shabbily between a prie-dieu and the tarnished hangings of his bed; Mélusine, with the pale frosty hair of a child, spins the melancholy of departed passion; Ahasuerus the Jew buys Melicent for a hundred and two minæ and enters her room past midnight for his act of abnegation. And at the end, looking, perhaps, for a mortal woman, Perion finds, in a flesh not unscarred by years, the rose beyond destruction, the high silver flame of immortal happiness.

So much, then, everything in the inner questioning of beings condemned to a glimpse of remote perfection, as though the sky had opened on a city of pure bliss, transpires in *Domnei;* while the fact that it is laid in Poictesme sharpens the thrust of its illusion. It is by that much the easier of entry; it borders—rather than on the clamor of mills—on the reaches men explore, leaving weariness and dejection for fancy—a geography for lonely sensibilities betrayed by chance into the blind traps, the issueless barrens, of existence.

JOSEPH HERGESHEIMER.

CRITICAL COMMENT

And Norman NICOLAS *at hearté meant*
(Pardie!) some subtle occupation
In making of his Tale of Melicent,
That stubbornly desiréd Perion.
What perils for to rollen up and down,
So long process, so many a sly cautel,
For to obtain a silly damosel!

—THOMAS UPCLIFFE.

Critical Comment

NICOLAS DE CAEN, one of the most eminent of the early French writers of romance, was born at Caen in Normandy early in the 15th century, and was living in 1470. Little is known of his life, apart from the fact that a portion of his youth was spent in England, where he was connected in some minor capacity with the household of the Queen Dowager, Joan of Navarre. In later life, from the fact that two of his works are dedicated to Isabella of Portugal, third wife to Philip the Good, Duke of Burgundy, it is conjectured that Nicolas was attached to the court of that prince. . . . Nicolas de Caen was not greatly esteemed nor highly praised by his contemporaries, or by writers of the century following, but latterly has received the recognition due to his unusual qualities of invention and conduct of narrative, together with his considerable knowledge of men and manners, and occasional remarkable modernity of thought. His books, therefore, apart from the interest attached to them as specimens of early French romance, and in spite of the difficulties and crudities of the unformed language in which they are written, are still readable, and are rich in instructive detail concerning the age that gave them birth. . . . Many romances are attributed to Nicolas de Caen. Modern criticism has selected four only as undoubtedly his. These are—(1) *Les Aventures d'Adhelmar de Nointel,* a metrical romance, plainly of youthful composition, containing some seven thousand verses; (2) *Le Roy*

Amaury, well known to English students in Watson's spirited translation; (3) *Le Roman de Lusignan*, a re-handling of the Melusina myth, most of which is wholly lost; (4) *Le Dizain des Reines*, a collection of quasi-historical *novellino* interspersed with lyrics. Six other romances are known to have been written by Nicolas, but these have perished; and he is credited with the authorship of *Le Cocu Rouge*, included by Hinsauf, and of several Ovidian translations or imitations still unpublished. The Satires formerly attributed to him Bülg has shown to be spurious compositions of 17th century origin.

—E. NOEL CODMAN,
Handbook of Literary Pioneers.

Nicolas de Caen est un représentant agréable, naïf, et expressif de cet âge que nous aimons à nous représenter de loin comme l'âge d'or du bon vieux temps. . . . Nicolas croyait à son Roy et à sa Dame, il croyait surtout à son Dieu. Nicolas sentait que le monde était semé à chaque pas d'obscurités et d'embûches, et que l'inconnu était partout; partout aussi était le protecteur invisible et le soutien; à chaque souffle qui frémissait, Nicolas croyait le sentir comme derrière le rideau. Le ciel par-dessus ce Nicolas de Caen était ouvert, peuplé en chaque point de figures vivantes, de patrons attentifs et manifestes, d'une invocation directe. Le plus intrépide guerrier alors marchait dans un mélange habituel de crainte et de confiance, comme un tout petit enfant. A cette vue, les esprits les plus émancipés d'aujourd'hui ne sauraient s'empêcher de crier, en tempérant leur sourire par le respect: *Sancta simplicitas!*

—PAUL VERVILLE,
Notice sur la vie de Nicolas de Caen.

THE ARGUMENT

"Of how, through Woman-Worship, knaves compound
With honoure; Kings reck not of their domaine;
Proud Pontiffs sigh; & War-men world-renownd,
Toe win one Woman, all things else disdaine:
Since Melicent doth in herselfe contayne
All this world's Riches that may farre be found.

"If Saphyres ye desire, her eies are plaine;
If Rubies, loe, hir lips be Rubyes sound;
If Pearles, hir teeth be Pearles, both pure & round;
If Yvorie, her forehead Yvory weene;
If Gold, her locks with finest Gold abound;
If Silver, her faire hands have Silver's sheen.

"Yet that which fayrest is, but Few beholde,
Her Soul adornd with vertues manifold."

—Sir William Allonby.

PART ONE

PERION

How Perion, that stalwart was and gay,
Treadeth with sorrow on a holiday,
Since Melicent anon must wed a king:
How in his heart he hath vain love-longing,
For which he putteth life in forfeiture,
And would no longer in such wise endure;
For writhing Perion in Venus' fire
So burneth that he dieth for desire.

THE ROMANCE OF LUSIGNAN OF THAT FORGOTTEN MAKER IN THE FRENCH TONGUE, MESSIRE NICOLAS DE CAEN. HERE BEGINS THE TALE WHICH THEY OF POICTESME NARRATE CONCERNING DAME MELICENT, THAT WAS DAUGHTER TO THE GREAT COUNT MANUEL.

I.
How Perion Was Unmasked

PERION afterward remembered the two weeks spent at Bellegarde as in recovery from illness a person might remember some long fever-dream which was all of an intolerable elvish brightness and of incessant laughter everywhere. They made a deal of him in Count Emmerick's pleasant home: day by day the outlaw was thrust into relations of mirth with noblemen, proud ladies, and even with a king; and was all the while half lightheaded through his singular knowledge as to how precariously the self-styled Vicomte de Puysange now balanced himself, as it were, upon a gilded stepping-stone from infamy to oblivion.

Now that King Theodoret had withdrawn his sinister presence, young Perion spent some seven hours of every day alone, to all intent, with Dame Melicent. There might be merry people within a stone's throw, about this recreation or another, but these two seemed to watch aloofly, as royal persons do the antics of their hired comedians, without any condescension into open interest. They were together; and the jostle of earthly happenings might hope, at most, to afford them matter for incurious comment.

They sat, as Perion thought, for the last time together, part of an audience before which the Confraternity of St. Médard was enacting a masque of *The Birth of Hercules.* The Bishop of Montors had returned to Bellegarde that evening with his brother, Count Gui, and the pleasure-loving prelate had brought these mirth-makers in his train. Clad in scarlet, he rode before them playing upon a lute—unclerical conduct which shocked his preciser brother and surprised nobody.

In such circumstances Perion began to speak with an odd purpose, because his reason was bedrugged by the beauty and purity of Melicent, and perhaps a little by the slow and clutching music to whose progress the chorus of Theban virgins was dancing. When he had made an end of harsh whispering, Melicent sat for a while in scrupulous appraisement of the rushes. The music was so sweet it seemed to Perion he must go mad unless she spoke within the moment.

Then Melicent said:

"You tell me you are not the Vicomte de Puysange. You tell me you are, instead, the late King Helmas' servitor, suspected of his murder. You are the fellow that stole the royal jewels—the outlaw for whom half Christendom is searching—"

Thus Melicent began to speak at last; and still he could not intercept those huge and tender eyes whose purple made the thought of heaven comprehensible.

The man replied:

"I am that widely hounded Perion of the Forest. The true vicomte is the wounded rascal over whose delirium we marvelled only last Tuesday. Yes, at the door of your home I attacked him, fought him —hah, but fairly, madame!—and stole his brilliant garments and with them his papers. Then in my desperate necessity I dared to masquerade. For I know enough about dancing to estimate that to dance upon air must necessarily prove to everybody a disgusting performance, but pre-eminently unpleasing to the main actor. Two weeks of safety till the *Tranchemer* sailed I therefore valued at a perhaps preposterous rate. To-night, as I have said, the ship lies at anchor off Manneville."

Melicent said an odd thing, asking, "Oh, can it be

you are a less despicable person than you are striving to appear!"

"Rather, I am a more unmitigated fool than even I suspected, since when affairs were in a promising train I have elected to blurt out, of all things, the naked and distasteful truth. Proclaim it now; and see the late Vicomte de Puysange lugged out of this hall and after appropriate torture hanged within the month." And with that Perion laughed.

Thereafter he was silent. As the masque went, Amphitryon had newly returned from warfare, and was singing under Alcmena's window in the terms of an aubade, a waking-song. *"Rei glorios, verais lums e clardatz—"* Amphitryon had begun. Dame Melicent heard him through.

And after many ages, as it seemed to Perion, the soft and brilliant and exquisite mouth was pricked to motion.

"You have affronted, by an incredible imposture and beyond the reach of mercy, every listener in this hall. You have injured me most deeply of all persons here. Yet it is to me alone that you confess."

Perion leaned forward. You are to understand that, through the incurrent necessities of every circumstance, each of them spoke in whispers, even now. It was curious to note the candid mirth on either side. Mercury was making his adieux to Alcmena's waiting-woman in the middle of a jig.

"But you," sneered Perion, "are merciful in all things. Rogue that I am, I dare to build on this notorious fact. I am snared in a hard golden trap, I cannot get a guide to Manneville, I cannot even procure a horse from Count Emmerick's stables without arousing fatal suspicions; and I must be at Manneville by dawn or else be hanged. Therefore I dare stake all upon one throw; and you must either save or hang me with unwashed hands. As surely as God reigns, my future rests with you. And as I am perfectly aware, you could not live comfortably with a gnat's death upon your conscience. Eh, am I not a seasoned rascal?"

"Do not remind me now that you are vile," said Melicent. "Ah, no, not now!"

"Lackey, impostor, and thief!" he sternly answered. "There you have the catalogue of all my rightful titles. And besides, it pleases me, for a reason I cannot entirely fathom, to be unpardonably candid and to fling my destiny into your lap. To-night, as I have said, the *Tranchemer* lies off Manneville; keep counsel, get me a horse if you will, and to-morrow I am embarked for desperate service under the harried Kaiser of the Greeks, and for throat-cuttings from which I am not likely ever to return. Speak, and I hang before the month is up."

Dame Melicent looked at him now, and within the moment Perion was repaid, and bountifully, for every folly and misdeed of his entire life.

"What harm have I ever done you, Messire de la Forêt, that you should shame me in this fashion? Until to-night I was not unhappy in the belief I was loved by you. I may say that now without paltering, since you are not the man I thought some day to love. You are but the rind of him. And you would force me to cheat justice, to become a hunted thief's accomplice, or else to murder you!"

"It comes to that, madame."

"Then I must help you preserve your life by any sorry stratagems you may devise. I shall not hinder you. I will procure you a guide to Manneville. I will even forgive you all save one offence, since doubtless heaven made you the foul thing you are." The girl was in a hot and splendid rage. "For you love me. Women know. You love me. You!"

"Undoubtedly, madame."

"Look into my face! and say what horrid writ of

infamy you fancied was apparent there, that my nails may destroy it."

"I am all base," he answered, "and yet not so profoundly base as you suppose. Nay, believe me, I had never hoped to win even such scornful kindness as you might accord your lapdog. I have but dared to peep at heaven while I might, and only as lost Dives peeped. Ignoble as I am, I never dreamed to squire an angel down toward the mire and filth which is henceforward my inevitable kennel."

"The masque is done," said Melicent, "and yet you talk, and talk, and talk, and mimic truth so cunningly— Well, I will send some trusty person to you. And now, for God's sake!—nay, for the fiend's love who is your patron!—let me not ever see you again, Messire de la Forêt."

2.

How the Vicomte Was Very Gay

THERE was dancing afterward and a sumptuous supper. The Vicomte de Puysange was generally accounted that evening the most excellent of company. He mingled affably with the revellers and found a prosperous answer for every jest they broke upon the projected marriage of Dame Melicent and King Theodoret; and meanwhile hugged the reflection that half the realm was hunting Perion de la Forêt in the more customary haunts of rascality. The springs of Perion's turbulent mirth were that to-morrow every person in the room would discover how impudently every person had been tricked, and that Melicent deliberated even now, and could not but admire, the hunted outlaw's insolence, however much she loathed its perpetrator; and over this thought in particular Perion laughed like a madman.

"You are very gay to-night, Messire de Puysange," said the Bishop of Montors.

This remarkable young man, it is necessary to repeat, had reached Bellegarde that evening, coming from Brunbelois. It was he (as you have heard) who had arranged the match with Theodoret. The bishop himself loved his cousin Melicent; but, now that he was in holy orders and possession of her had become impossible, he had cannily resolved to utilise her beauty, as he did everything else, toward his own preferment.

"Oh, sir," replied Perion, "you who are so fine a poet must surely know that *gay* rhymes with *to-day* as patly as *sorrow* goes with *to-morrow*."

"Yet your gay laughter, Messire de Puysange, is after all but breath: and *breath* also"—the bishop's sharp eyes fixed Perion's—"has a hackneyed rhyme."

"Indeed, it is the grim rhyme that rounds off and silences all our rhyming," Perion assented. "I must laugh, then, without rhyme or reason."

Still the young prelate talked rather oddly. "But," said he, "you have an excellent reason, now that you sup so near to heaven." And his glance at Melicent did not lack pith.

"No, no, I have quite another reason," Perion answered; "it is that to-morrow I breakfast in hell."

"Well, they tell me the landlord of that place is

used to cater to each according to his merits," the bishop, shrugging, returned.

And Perion thought how true this was when, at the evening's end, he was alone in his own room. His life was tolerably secure. He trusted Ahasuerus the Jew to see to it that, about dawn, one of the ship's boats would touch at Fomor Beach near Manneville, according to their old agreement. Aboard the *Tranchemer* the Free Companions awaited their captain; and the savage land they were bound for was a thought beyond the reach of a kingdom's lamentable curiosity concerning the whereabouts of King Helmas' treasure. The worthless life of Perion was safe.

For worthless, and far less than worthless, life seemed to Perion as he thought of Melicent and waited for her messenger. He thought of her beauty and purity and illimitable loving-kindness toward every person in the world save only Perion of the Forest. He thought of how clean she was in every thought and deed; of that, above all, he thought, and he knew that he would never see her any more.

"Oh, but past any doubting," said Perion, "the devil caters to each according to his merits."

3.
How Melicent Wooed

THEN Perion knew that vain regret had turned his brain, very certainly, for it seemed the door had opened and Dame Melicent herself had come, warily, into the panelled gloomy room. It seemed that Melicent paused in the convulsive brilliancy of the firelight, and stayed thus with vaguely troubled eyes like those of a child newly wakened from sleep.

And it seemed a long while before she told Perion very quietly that she had confessed all to Ayrart de Montors, and had, by reason of de Montors' love for her, so goaded and allured the outcome of their talk—"ignobly," as she said,—that a clean-handed gentleman would come at three o'clock for Perion de la Forêt, and guide a thief toward unmerited impunity. All this she spoke quite levelly, as one reads aloud from a book; and then, with a signal change of voice, Melicent said: "Yes, that is true enough. Yet why, in reality, do you think I have in my own person come to tell you of it?"

"Madame, I may not guess. Hah, indeed, indeed," Perion cried, because he knew the truth and was unspeakably afraid, "I dare not guess!"

"You sail to-morrow for the fighting oversea—" she began, but her sweet voice trailed and died into silence. He heard the crepitations of the fire, and even the hurried beatings of his own heart, as against a terrible and lovely hush of all created life. "Then take me with you."

Perion had never any recollection of what he answered. Indeed, he uttered no communicative words, but only foolish babblements.

"Oh, I do not understand," said Melicent. "It is as though some spell were laid upon me. Look you, I have been cleanly reared, I have never wronged any person that I know of, and throughout my quiet, sheltered life I have loved truth and honour most of all. My judgment grants you to be what you are confessedly. And there is that in me more masterful and surer than my judgment, that which seems omniscient and lightly puts aside your confessings as unimportant."

"Lackey, impostor, and thief!" young Perion answered. "There you have the catalogue of all my rightful titles fairly earned."

"And even if I believed you, I think I would not care! Is that not strange? For then I should despise you. And even then, I think, I would fling my honour at your feet, as I do now, and but in part with loathing, I would still entreat you to make of me your wife, your servant, anything that pleased you. . . . Oh, I had thought that when love came it would be sweet!"

Strangely quiet, in every sense, he answered:

"It is very sweet. I have known no happier moment in my life. For you stand within arm's reach, mine to touch, mine to possess and do with as I elect. And I dare not lift a finger. I am as a man that has lain for a long while in a dungeon vainly hungering for the glad light of day—who, being freed at last, must hide his eyes from the dear sunlight he dare not look upon as yet. Ho, I am past speech unworthy of your notice! and I pray you now speak harshly with me, madame, for when your pure eyes regard me kindly, and your bright and delicate lips have come thus near to mine, I am so greatly tempted and so happy that I fear lest heaven grow jealous!"

"Be not too much afraid—" she murmured.

"Nay, should I then be bold? and within the moment wake Count Emmerick to say to him, very boldly, 'Beau sire, the thief half Christendom is hunting has the honour to request your sister's hand in marriage'?"

"You sail to-morrow for the fighting oversea. Take me with you."

"Indeed the feat would be worthy of me. For you are a lady tenderly nurtured and used to every luxury the age affords. There comes to woo you presently an excellent and potent monarch, not all unworthy of your love, who will presently share with you many happy and honourable years. Yonder is a lawless naked wilderness where I and my fellow desperadoes hope to cheat offended justice and to preserve thrice-forfeited lives in savagery. You bid me aid you to go into this country, never to return! Madame, if I obeyed you, Satan would protest against pollution of his ageless fires by any soul so filthy."

"You talk of little things, whereas I think of great things. Love is not sustained by palatable food alone, and is not served only by those persons who go about the world in satin."

"Then take the shameful truth. It is undeniable I swore I loved you, and with appropriate gestures, too. But, dompnedex, madame! I am past master in these specious ecstasies, for somehow I have rarely seen the woman who had not some charm or other to catch my heart with. I confess now that you alone have never quickened it. My only purpose was through hyperbole to wheedle you out of a horse, and meanwhile to have my recreation, you handsome jade!—and that is all you ever meant to me. I swear to you that is all, all, all!" sobbed Perion, for it appeared that he must die. "I have amused myself with you, I have abominably tricked you—"

Melicent only waited with untroubled eyes which seemed to plumb his heart and to appraise all which Perion had ever thought or longed for since the day that Perion was born; and she was as beautiful, it seemed to him, as the untroubled, gracious angels are, and more compassionate.

"Yes," Perion said, "I am trying to lie to you. And even at lying I fail."

She said, with a wonderful smile:

"Assuredly there were never any other persons so mad as we. For I must do the wooing, as though you were the maid, and all the while you rebuff me and suffer so that I fear to look on you. Men say you are no better than a highwayman; you confess yourself to be a thief: and I believe none of your accusers. Perion de la Forêt," said Melicent, and ballad-makers have never shaped a phrase wherewith to tell you of her voice, "I know that you have dabbled in dishonour no more often than an archangel has pilfered drying linen from a hedgerow. I do not guess, for my hour is upon me, and inevitably I know! and there is nothing dares to come between us now."

"Nay,—ho, and even were matters as you suppose them, without any warrant,—there is at least one silly stumbling knave that dares as much. Saith he: 'What is the most precious thing in the world? —Why, assuredly, Dame Melicent's welfare. Let me get the keeping of it, then. For I have been entrusted with a host of common priceless things—with youth and vigour and honour, with a clean conscience and a child's faith, and so on—and no person alive has squandered them more gallantly. So heartward ho! and trust me now, my timorous yokefellow, to win and squander also the chiefest jewel of the world.' Eh, thus he chuckles and nudges me, with wicked whisperings. Indeed, madame, this rascal that shares equally in my least faculty is a most pitiful, ignoble rogue! and he has aforetime eked out our common livelihood by such practices as your unsullied imagination could scarcely depicture. Until I knew you I had endured him. But you have made of him a horror. A horror, a horror! a thing too pitiful for hell!"

Perion turned away from her, groaning. He flung himself into a chair. He screened his eyes as if before some physical abomination.

The girl kneeled close to him, touching him. "My dear, my dear! then slay for me this other Perion of the Forest."

And Perion laughed, not very mirthfully.

"It is the common usage of women to ask of men this little labour, which is a harder task than ever Hercules, that mighty-muscled king of heathenry, achieved. Nay, I, for all my sinews, am an attested weakling. The craft of other men I do not fear, for I have encountered no formidable enemy save myself; but that same midnight stabber unhorsed me long ago. I had wallowed in the mire contentedly enough until you came. . . . Ah, child, child! why needed you to trouble me! for to-night I want to be clean as you are clean, and that I may not ever be. I am garrisoned with devils, I am the battered plaything of every vice, and I lack the strength, and it may be, even the will, to leave my mire. Always I have betrayed the stewardship of man and god alike that my body might escape a momentary discomfort! And loving you as I do, I cannot swear that in the outcome I would not betray you too, to this same end! I cannot swear— Oh, now let Satan laugh, yet not unpitifully, since he and I, alone, know all the reasons why I may not swear! Hah, Madame Melicent!" cried Perion, in his great agony, "you offer me that gift an emperor might not accept save in awed gratitude; and I refuse it." Gently he raised her to her feet. "And now, in God's name, go, madame, and leave the prodigal among his husks."

"You are a very brave and foolish gentleman," she said, "who chooses to face his own achievements without any paltering. To every man, I think, that must be bitter work; to the woman who loves him it is impossible."

Perion could not see her face, because he lay prone at the feet of Melicent, sobbing, but without any tears, and tasting very deeply of such grief and vain regret as, he had thought, they know in hell alone; and even after she had gone, in silence, he lay in this same posture for an exceedingly long while.

And after he knew not how long a while, Perion propped his chin between his hands and, still sprawling upon the rushes, stared hard into the little, crackling fire. He was thinking of a Perion de la Forêt that once had been. In him might have been found a fit mate for Melicent had this boy not died very long ago.

It is no more cheerful than any other mortuary employment, this disinterment of the person you have been, and are not any longer; and so did Perion find his cataloguing of irrevocable old follies and evasions.

Then Perion arose and looked for pen and ink. It was the first letter he ever wrote to Melicent, and, as you will presently learn, she never saw it.

In such terms Perion wrote:

"Madame—It may please you to remember that when Dame Mélusine and I were interrogated, I freely confessed to the murder of King Helmas and the theft of my dead master's jewels. In that I lied. For it was my manifest duty to save the woman whom, as I thought, I loved, and it was apparent that the guilty person was either she or I.

"She is now at Brunbelois, where, as I have heard, the splendour of her estate is tolerably notorious. I have not ever heard she gave a thought to me, her cat's-paw. Madame, when I think of you and then of that sleek, smiling woman, I am appalled by my own folly. I am aghast by my long blindness as I write the words which no one will believe. To what avail do I deny a crime which every circumstance imputed to me and my own confession has publicly acknowledged?

"But you, I think, will believe me. Look you, madame, I have nothing to gain of you. I shall not ever see you any more. I go into a perilous and an eternal banishment; and in the immediate neighbourhood of death a man finds little sustenance for romance. Take the worst of me: a gentleman I was born, and as a wastrel I have lived, and always very foolishly; but without dishonour. I have never to my knowledge—and God judge me as I speak the truth!—wronged any man or woman save myself. My dear, believe me! believe me, in spite of reason! and understand that my adoration and misery and unworthiness when I think of you are such as I cannot measure, and afford me no judicious moment wherein to fashion lies. For I shall not see you any more.

"I thank you, madame, for your all-unmerited kindnesses, and, oh, I pray you to believe!"

4.
How the Bishop Aided Perion

THEN at three o'clock, as Perion supposed, someone tapped upon the door. Perion went out into the corridor, which was now unlighted, so that he had to hold to the cloak of Ayrart de Montors as the young prelate guided Perion through the complexities of unfamiliar halls and stairways into an inhospitable night. There were ready two horses, and presently the men were mounted and away.

Once only Perion shifted in the saddle to glance back at Bellegarde, black and formless against an empty sky; and he dared not look again, for the thought of her that lay awake in the Marshal's Tower, so near at hand as yet, was like a dagger. With set teeth he followed in the wake of his taciturn companion. The bishop never spoke save to growl out some direction.

Thus they came to Manneville and, skirting the

town, came to Fomor Beach, a narrow sandy coast. It was dark in this place and very still save for the encroachment of the tide. Yonder were four little lights, lazily heaving with the water's motion, to show them where the *Tranchemer* lay at anchor. It did not seem to Perion that anything mattered.

"It will be nearing dawn by this," he said.

"Ay," Ayrart de Montors said, very briefly; and his tone evinced his willingness to dispense with further conversation. Perion of the Forest was an unclean thing which the bishop must touch in his necessity, but could touch with loathing only, as a thirsty man takes a fly out of his drink. Perion conceded it, because nothing would ever matter any more; and so, the horses tethered, they sat upon the sand in utter silence for the space of a half hour.

A bird cried somewhere, just once, and with a start Perion knew the night was not quite so murky as it had been, for he could now see a broken line of white, where the tide crept up and shattered and ebbed. Then in a while a light sank tipsily to the water's level and presently was bobbing in the darkness, apart from those other lights, and it was growing in size and brilliancy.

Said Perion, "They have sent out the boat."

"Ay," the bishop answered, as before.

A sort of madness came upon Perion, and it seemed that he must weep, because everything fell out so very ill in this world.

"Messire de Montors, you have aided me. I would be grateful if you permitted it."

De Montors spoke at last, saying crisply:

"Gratitude, I take it, forms no part of the bargain. I am the kinsman of Dame Melicent. It makes for my interest and for the honour of our house that the man whose rooms she visits at night be got out of Poictesme—"

Said Perion, "You speak in this fashion of the most lovely lady God has made—of her whom the world adores!"

"Adores!" the bishop answered, with a laugh; "and what poor gull am I to adore an attested wanton?" Then, with a sneer, he spoke of Melicent, and in such terms as are not bettered by repetition.

Perion said:

"I am the most unhappy man alive, as surely as you are the most ungenerous. For, look you, in my presence you have spoken infamy of Dame Melicent, though knowing I am in your debt so deeply that I have not the right to resent anything you may elect to say. You have just given me my life; and armoured by the fire-new obligation, you blaspheme an angel, you condescend to buffet a fettered man—"

But with that his sluggish wits had spied an honest way out of the imbroglio.

Perion said then, "Draw, messire! for, as God lives, I may yet repurchase, at this eleventh hour, the privilege of destroying you."

"Heyday! but here is an odd evincement of gratitude!" de Montors retorted; "and though I am not particularly squeamish, let me tell you, my fine fellow, I do not ordinarily fight with lackeys."

"Nor are you fit to do so, messire. Believe me, there is not a lackey in this realm—no, not a cut-purse, nor any pander—who would not in meeting you upon equal footing degrade himself. For you have slandered that which is most perfect in the world; yet lies, Messire de Montors, have short legs; and I design within the hour to insure the calumny against an echo."

"Rogue, I have given you your very life within the hour—"

"The fact is undeniable. Thus I must fling the bounty back to you, so that we sorry scoundrels may meet as equals." Perion wheeled toward the boat, which was now within the reach of wading. "Who is among you? Gaucelm, Roger, Jean Britauz—" He found the man he sought. "Ahasuerus, the captain that was to have accompanied the Free Companions oversea is of another mind. I cede my leadership to Landry de Bonnay. You will have the kindness to inform him of the unlooked-for change, and to tender your new captain every appropriate regret and the dying felicitations of Perion de la Forêt."

He bowed toward the landward twilight, where the sand hillocks were taking form.

"Messire de Montors, we may now resume our vigil. When yonder vessel sails there will be no conceivable happening that can keep breath within my body two weeks longer. I shall be quit of every debt to you. You will then fight with a man already dead if you so elect; but otherwise—if you attempt to flee this place, if you decline to cross swords with a lackey, with a convicted thief, with a suspected murderer, I swear upon my mother's honour! I will demolish you without compunction, as I would any other vermin."

"Oh, brave, brave!" sneered the bishop, "to fling away your life, and perhaps mine too, for an idle word—" But at that he fetched a sob. "How foolish of you! and how like you!" he said, and Perion wondered at this prelate's voice.

"Hey, gentlemen!" cried Ayrart de Montors, "a moment if you please!" He splashed kneedeep into the icy water, wading to the boat, where he snatched the lantern from the Jew's hands and fetched this light ashore. He held it aloft, so that Perion might see his face, and Perion perceived that, by some wonder-working, the person in man's attire who held this light aloft was Melicent. It was odd that Perion always remembered afterward most clearly of all the loosened wisp of hair the wind tossed about her forehead.

"Look well upon me, Perion," said Melicent. "Look well, ruined gentleman! look well, poor hunted vagabond! and note how proud I am. Oh, in all things I am very proud! A little I exult in my high station and in my wealth, and, yes, even in my beauty, for I know that I am beautiful, but it is the chief of all my honours that you love me—and so foolishly!"

"You do not understand—!" cried Perion.

"Rather I understand at last that you are in sober verity a lackey, an impostor, and a thief, even as you said. Ay, a lackey to your honour! an impostor that would endeavour—and, oh, so very vainly!—to impersonate another's baseness! and a thief that has stolen another person's punishment! I ask no questions; loving means trusting; but I would like to kill that other person very, very slowly. I ask no questions, but I dare to trust the man I know of, even in defiance of that man's own voice. I dare protest the man no thief, but in all things a madly honourable gentleman. My poor bruised, puzzled boy," said Melicent, with an odd mirthful tenderness, "how came you to be blundering about this miry world of ours! Only be very good for my sake and forget the bitterness; what does it matter when there is happiness, too?"

He answered nothing, but it was not because of misery.

"Come, come, will you not even help me into the boat?" said Melicent. She, too, was glad.

5.

How Melicent Wedded

"THAT may not be, my cousin."

It was the real Bishop of Montors who was speaking. His company, some fifteen men in all, had ridden up while Melicent and Perion looked seaward. The bishop was clothed, in his habitual fashion, as a cavalier, showing in nothing as a churchman. He sat a-horseback for a considerable while, looking down at them, smiling and stroking the pommel of his saddle with a gold-fringed glove. It was now dawn.

"I have been eavesdropping," the bishop said. His voice was tender, for the young man loved his kinswoman with an affection second only to that which he reserved for Ayrart de Montors. "Yes, I have been eavesdropping for an instant, and through that instant I seemed to see the heart of every woman that ever lived; and they differed only as stars differ on a fair night in August. No woman ever loved a man except, at bottom, as a mother loves her child: let him elect to build a nation or to write imperishable verses or to take purses upon the highway, and she will only smile to note how breathlessly the boy goes about his playing; and when he comes back to her with grimier hands she is a little sorry, and, if she think it salutary, will pretend to be angry. Meanwhile she sets about the quickest way to cleanse him and to heal his bruises. They are more wise than we, and at the bottom of their hearts they pity us more stalwart folk whose grosser wits require, to be quite sure of anything, a mere crass proof of it; and always they make us better by indomitably believing we are better than in reality a man can ever be."

Now Ayrart de Montors dismounted.

"So much for my sermon. For the rest, Messire de la Forêt, I perfectly recognised you on the day you came to Bellegarde. But I said nothing. For that you had not murdered King Helmas, as is popularly reported, I was certain, inasmuch as I happen to know he is now at Brunbelois, where Dame Mélusine has put a mighty magic upon him. A terrible, delicious woman! begotten on a water-demon, people say. I ask no questions. She is a close and useful friend to me, and through her aid

I hope to go far. You see that I am frank. It is my nature." The bishop shrugged. "In a phrase, I accepted the Vicomte de Puysange, although it was necessary, of course, to keep an eye upon your comings in and your goings out, as you now see. And until this the imposture amused me. But this"—his hand waved toward the *Tranchemer*—"this, my fair friends, is past a jest."

"You talk and talk," cried Perion, "while I reflect that I love the fairest lady who at any time has had life upon earth."

"The proof of your affection," the bishop returned, "is, if you will permit the observation, somewhat extraordinary. For you propose, I gather, to make of her a camp-follower, a soldier's drab. Come, come, messire! you and I are conversant with warfare as it is. Armies do not conduct encounters by throwing sugar-candy at one another. What home have you, a landless man, to offer Melicent? What place is there for Melicent among your Free Companions?"

"Oh, do I not know that!" said Perion. He turned to Melicent, and long and long they gazed upon each other.

"Ignoble as I am," said Perion, "I never

dreamed to squire an angel down toward the mire and filth which for a while as yet must be my kennel. I go. I go alone. Do you bid me return?"

The girl was perfectly calm. She took a ring of diamonds from her hand, and placed it on his little finger, because the others were too large.

"While life endures I pledge you faith and service, Perion. There is no need to speak of love."

"There is no need," he answered. "Oh, does God think that I will live without you!"

"I suppose they will give me to King Theodoret. The terrible old man has set my body as the only price that will buy him off from ravaging Poictesme, and he is stronger in the field than Emmerick. Emmerick is afraid of him, and Ayrart here has need of the King's friendship in order to become a cardinal. So my kinsmen must make traffic of my eyes and lips and hair. But first I wed you, Perion, here in the sight of God, and I bid you return to me, who am your wife and servitor for ever now, whatever lesser men may do."

"I will return," he said.

Then in a little while she withdrew her lips from his lips.

"Cover my face, Ayrart. It may be I shall weep presently. Men must not see the wife of Perion weep. Cover my face, for he is going now, and I cannot watch his going."

PART TWO

MELICENT

Of how through love is Melicent upcast
Under a heathen castle at the last:
And how a wicked lord of proud degree,
Demetrios, dwelleth in this country,
Where humbled under him are all mankind:
How to this wretched woman he hath mind,
That fallen is in pagan lands alone,
In point to die, as presently is shown.

6.

How Melicent Sought Oversea

IT is a tale which they narrate in Poictesme, telling how love began between Perion of the Forest, who was a captain of mercenaries, and young Melicent, who was daughter to the great Dom Manuel, and sister to Count Emmerick of Poictesme. They tell also how Melicent and Perion were parted, because there was no remedy, and policy demanded she should wed King Theodoret.

And the tale tells how Perion sailed with his retainers to seek desperate service under the harried Kaiser of the Greeks.

This venture was ill-fated, since, as the Free Companions were passing not far from Masillia, their vessel being at the time becalmed, they were attacked by three pagan galleys under the admiralty of the proconsul Demetrios. Perion's men, who fought so hardily on land, were novices at sea. They were powerless against an adversary who, from a great distance, showered liquid fire upon their vessel.

Then Demetrios sent little boats and took some thirty prisoners from the blazing ship, and made slaves of all save Ahasuerus the Jew, whom he released on being informed of the lean man's religion. It was a customary boast of this Demetrios that he made war on Christians only.

And presently, as Perion had commanded, Ahasuerus came to Melicent.

The princess sat in a high chair, the back of which was capped with a big lion's head in brass. It gleamed above her head, but was less glorious than her bright hair.

Ahasuerus made dispassionate report. "Thus painfully I have delivered, as my task was, these fine messages concerning Faith and Love and Death and so on. Touching their rationality I may reserve my own opinion. I am merely Perion's echo. Do I echo madness? This madman was my loved and honoured master once, a lord without any peer in the fields where men contend in battle. To-day those sinews which preserved a throne are dedicated to the transportation of luggage. Grant it is laughable. I do not laugh."

"And I lack time to weep," said Melicent.

So, when the Jew had told his tale and gone, young Melicent arose and went into a chamber painted with the histories of Jason and Medea, where her brother Count Emmerick hid such jewels as had not many equals in Christendom.

She did not hesitate. She took no thought for Niafer her mother, nor any heed of her sisters: Ettarre and Dorothy were their names, and they also suffered for their beauty, and for the desire it quickened in the hearts of men. Melicent knew only that Perion was in captivity and might not look for aid from any person living save herself.

She gathered in a blue napkin such emeralds as would ransom a pope. She cut short her marvellous hair and disguised herself in all things as a man, and under cover of the ensuing night slipped from the castle. At Manneville she found a Venetian ship bound homeward with a cargo of swords and armour.

She hired herself to the captain of this vessel as a servant, calling herself Jocelin Gaignars. She found no time wherein to be afraid or to grieve for the estate she was relinquishing, so long as Perion lay in danger.

Thus the young Jocelin, though not without hardship and odd by-ends of adventure here irrelevant, came with time's course into a land of sunlight and much wickedness where Perion was.

There the boy found in what fashion Perion was living and won the dearly purchased misery of seeing him, from afar, in his deplorable condition, as Perion went through the outer yard of Nacumera laden with chains and carrying great logs toward the kitchen. This befell when Jocelin had come into the hill country, where the eyrie of Demetrios blocked a crag-hung valley as snugly as a stone chokes a gutter-pipe.

Young Jocelin had begged an audience of this heathen lord and had obtained it—though Jocelin did not know as much—with ominous facility.

7.
How Perion Was Freed

DEMETRIOS lay on a divan within the Court of Stars, through which you passed from the fortress into the Women's Garden and the luxurious prison where he kept his wives. This court was circular in form and was paved with red and yellow slabs, laid alternately, like a chess-board. In the centre was a fountain, which cast up a tall thin jet of water. A gallery extended around the place, supported by columns that had been painted scarlet and were gilded with fantastic designs. The walls were of the colour of claret and were adorned with golden cinquefoils regularly placed. From a distance they resembled stars, and so gave the enclosure its name.

Demetrios lay upon a long divan which was covered with crimson, and which encircled the court entirely, save for the apertures of the two entrances. Demetrios was of burly person, which he by ordinary, as to-day, adorned resplendently; of a stature little above the common size, and disproportionately broad as to his chest and shoulders. It was rumoured that he could bore an apple through with his forefinger and had once killed a refractory horse with a blow of his naked fist; nor looking on the man, did you presume to question the report. His eyes were large and insolent, coloured like onyxes; for the rest, he had a handsome surly face which was disfigured by pimples.

He did not speak at all while Jocelin explained that his errand was to ransom Perion. Then, "At what price?" Demetrios said, without any sign of interest; and Jocelin, with many encomiums, displayed his emeralds.

"Ay, they are well enough," Demetrios agreed. "But then I have a superfluity of jewels."

He raised himself a little among the cushions, and in this moving the figured golden stuff in which he was clothed heaved and glittered like the scales of a splendid monster. He leisurely unfastened the great chrysoberyl, big as a hen's egg, which adorned his fillet.

"Look you, this is of a far more beautiful green than any of your trinkets. I think it is as valuable also, because of its huge size. Moreover, it turns red by lamplight—red as blood. That is an admirable colour. And yet I do not value it. I think I do not value anything. So I will make you a gift of this big coloured pebble, if you desire it, because your ignorance amuses me. Most people know Demetrios is not a merchant. He does not buy and sell. That which he has he keeps, and that which he desires he takes."

The boy was all despair. He did not speak. He was very handsome as he stood in that still place where everything excepting him was red and gold.

"You do not value my poor chrysoberyl? You value your friend more? It is a page out of Theocritos—'when there were golden men of old, when friends gave love for love.' And yet I could have sworn— Come now, a wager," purred Demetrios. "Show your contempt of this bauble to be as great as mine by throwing this shiny pebble, say, into the gallery, for the next passer-by to pick up, and I will credit your sincerity. Do that and I will even name my price for Perion."

The boy obeyed him without hesitation. Turning, he saw the horrid change in the intent eyes of Demetrios, and quailed before it. But instantly that flare of passion flickered out.

Demetrios gently said:

"A bargain is a bargain. My wives are beautiful, but their caresses annoy me as much as formerly they pleased me. I have long thought it would perhaps amuse me if I possessed a Christian wife who had eyes like violets and hair like gold, and a plump white body. A man tires very soon of ebony and amber. . . . Procure me such a wife and I will willingly release this Perion and all his fellows who are yet alive."

"But, seignior,"—and the boy was shaken now,—"you demand of me an impossibility!"

"I am so hardy as to think not. And my reason is that a man throws from the elbow only, but a woman with her whole arm."

There fell a silence now.

"Why, look you, I deal fairly, though. Were such a woman here—Demetrios of Anatolia's guest—I verily believe I would not hinder her departure, as I might easily do. For there is not a person within many miles of this place who considers it wholesome to withstand me. Yet were this woman purchasable, I would purchase. And—if she refused—I would not hinder her departure; but very certainly I would put Perion to the Torment of the Waterdrops. It is so droll to see a man go mad before your eyes, I think that I would laugh and quite forget the woman."

She said, "O God, I cry to You for justice!"

He answered:

"My good girl, in Nacumera the wishes of Demetrios are justice. But we waste time. You desire to purchase one of my belongings? So be it. I will hear your offer."

Just once her hands had gripped each other. Her arms fell now as if they had been drained of life. She spoke in a dull voice.

"Seignior, I offer Melicent who was a princess. I cry a price, seignior, for red lips and bright eyes and a fair woman's tender body without any blemish. I cry a price for youth and happiness and honour. These you may have for playthings, seignior, with everything which I possess, except my heart, for that is dead."

Demetrios asked, "Is this true speech?"

She answered:

"It is as sure as Love and Death. I know that nothing is more sure than these, and I praise God for my sure knowledge."

He chuckled, saying, "Platitudes break no bones."

So on the next day the chains were filed from

Perion de la Forêt and all his fellows, save the nine unfortunates whom Demetrios had appointed to fight with lions a month before this, when he had entertained the Soldan of Bacharia. These men were bathed and perfumed and richly clad.

A galley of the proconsul's fleet conveyed them toward Christendom and set the twoscore slaves of yesterday ashore not far from Megaris. The captain of the galley on departure left with Perion a blue napkin, wherein were wrapped large emeralds and a bit of parchment.

Upon this parchment was written:

"Not these, but the body of Melicent, who was once a princess, purchased your bodies. Yet these will buy you ships and men and swords with which to storm my house where Melicent now is. Come if you will and fight with Demetrios of Anatolia for that brave girl who loved a porter as all loyal men should love their Maker and customarily do not. I think it would amuse us."

Then Perion stood by the languid sea which severed him from Melicent and cried:

"O God, that hast permitted this hard bargain, trade now with me! now barter with me, O Father of us all! That which a man has I will give."

Thus he waited in the clear sunlight, with no more

wavering in his face than you may find in the next statue's face. Both hands strained toward the blue sky, as though he made a vow. If so, he did not break it.

And now no more of Perion.

At the same hour young Melicent, wrapped all about with a flame-coloured veil and crowned with marjoram, was led by a spruce boy toward a threshold, over which Demetrios lifted her, while many people sang in a strange tongue. And then she paid her ransom.

"Hymen, O Hymen!" they sang. "Do thou of many names and many temples, golden Aphrodite, be propitious to this bridal! Now let him first compute the glittering stars of midnight and the grasshoppers of a summer day who would count the joys this bridal shall bring about! Hymen, O Hymen, rejoice thou in this bridal!"

8.

How Demetrios Was Amused

NOW Melicent abode in the house of Demetrios, whom she had not seen since the morning after he had wedded her. A month had passed. As yet she could not understand the language of her fellow prisoners, but Halaon, a eunuch who had once served a cardinal in Tuscany, informed her the proconsul was in the West Provinces, where an invading force had landed under Ranulph de Meschines.

A month had passed. She woke one night from dreams of Perion—what else should women dream of?—and found the same Ahasuerus that had brought her news of Perion's captivity, so long ago, attendant at her bedside.

He seemed a prey to some half-scornful mirth. In speech, at least, the man was of entire discretion. "The Splendour of the World desires your presence, madame." Thus the Jew blandly spoke.

She cried, aghast at so much treachery, "You had planned this!"

He answered:

"I plan always. Oh, certainly, I must weave always as the spider does. . . . Meanwhile time passes. I, like you, am now the servitor of Demetrios. I am his factor now at Calonak. I buy and sell. I estimate ounces. I earn my wages. Who forbids it?" Here the Jew shrugged. "And to conclude, the Splendour of the World desires your presence, madame."

He seemed to get much joy of this mouth-filling periphrasis as sneeringly he spoke of their common master.

Now Melicent, in a loose robe of green Coan stuff shot through and through with a radiancy like that of copper, followed the thin, smiling Jew Ahasuerus. She came thus with bare feet into the Court of Stars, where the proconsul lay on the divan as though he had not ever moved from there. To-night he was clothed in scarlet, and barbaric ornaments dangled from his pierced ears. These glittered now that his head moved a little as he silently dismissed Ahasuerus from the Court of Stars.

Real stars were overhead, so brilliant and (it

seemed) so near they turned the fountain's jet into a spurt of melting silver. The moon was set, but there was a flaring lamp of iron, high as a man's shoulder, yonder where Demetrios lay.

"Stand close to it, my wife," said the proconsul, "in order that I may see my newest purchase very clearly."

She obeyed him; and she esteemed the sacrifice, however unendurable, which bought for Perion the chance to serve God and his love for her by valorous and commendable actions to be no cause for grief.

"I think with those old men who sat upon the walls of Troy," Demetrios said, and he laughed because his voice had shaken a little. "Meanwhile I have returned from crucifying a hundred of your fellow worshippers," Demetrios continued. His speech had an odd sweetness. "Ey, yes, I conquered at Yroga. It was a good fight. My horse's hoofs were red at its conclusion. My surviving opponents I consider to have been deplorable fools when they surrendered, for people die less painfully in battle. There was one fellow, a Franciscan monk, who hung six hours upon a palm tree, always turning his head from one side to the other. It was amusing."

She answered nothing.

"And I was wondering always how I would feel were you nailed in his place. It was curious I should have thought of you. . . . But your white flesh is like the petals of a flower. I suppose it is as readily destructible. I think you would not long endure."

"I pray God hourly that I may not!" said tense Melicent.

He was pleased to have wrung one cry of anguish from this lovely effigy. He motioned her to him and laid one hand upon her naked breast. He gave a gesture of distaste.

Demetrios said:

"No, you are not afraid. However, you are very beautiful. I thought that you would please me more when your gold hair had grown a trifle longer. There is nothing in the world so beautiful as golden hair. Its beauty weathers even the commendation of poets."

No power of motion seemed to be in this white girl, but certainly you could detect no fear. Her clinging robe shone like an opal in the lamplight, her body, only partly veiled, was enticing, and her visage was very lovely. Her wide-open eyes implored you, but only as those of a trapped animal beseech the mercy for which it does not really hope. Thus Melicent waited in the clear lamplight, with no more wavering in her face than you may find in the next statue's face.

In the man's heart woke now some comprehension of the nature of her love for Perion, of that high and alien madness which dared to make of Demetrios of Anatolia's will an unavoidable discomfort, and no more. The prospect was alluring. The proconsul began to chuckle as water pours from a jar, and the gold in his ears twinkled.

"Decidedly I shall get much mirth of you. Go back to your own rooms. I had thought the world afforded no adversary and no game worthy of Demetrios. I have found both, in the daughter of that so famous Dom Manuel who, in his day and turn, afforded to my father, famous Miramon Lluagor, another sort of diversion. Therefore do you go back to your own rooms!"

9.
How Time Sped in Heathenry

ON the next day Melicent was removed to more magnificent apartments, and she was lodged in a lofty and spacious pavilion, which had three porticoes builded of marble and carved teakwood and Andalusian copper. Her rooms were spread with gold-worked carpets and hung with tapestries and brocaded silks figured with all manner of beasts and birds in their proper colours. Such was the girl's home now, where only happiness was denied to her. Many slaves attended Melicent, and she lacked for nothing in luxury and riches and things of price; and thereafter she abode at Nacumera, to all appearances, as the favourite among the proconsul's wives.

It must be recorded of Demetrios that henceforth he scrupulously demurred even to touch her. "I have purchased your body," he proudly said, "and I have taken seizin. I find I do not care for anything which can be purchased."

It may be that the man was never sane; it is indisputable that the mainspring of his least action was an inordinate pride. Here he had stumbled upon something which made of Demetrios of Anatolia a temporary discomfort, and which bedwarfed the utmost reach of his ill-doing into equality with the molestations of a house-fly; and perception of this fact worked in Demetrios like a poisonous ferment. To beg or once again to pillage he thought equally unworthy of himself. "Let us have patience!" It was not easily said so long as this fair Frankish woman dared to entertain a passion which Demetrios could not comprehend, and of which Demetrios was, and knew himself to be, incapable.

A connoisseur of passions, he resented such belittlement tempestuously; and he heaped every luxury upon Melicent, because, as he assured himself, the heart of every woman is alike.

He had his theories, his cunning, and, chief of all, an appreciation of her beauty, as his abettors. She had her memories and her clean heart. They duelled thus accoutred.

Meanwhile his other wives peered from screened alcoves at these two and duly hated Melicent. Upon no less than three occasions did Callistion—the first wife of the proconsul and the mother of his elder son—attempt the life of Melicent; and thrice Demetrios spared the woman at Melicent's entreaty. For Melicent (since she loved Perion) could understand that it was love of Demetrios, rather than hate of her, which drove the Dacian virago to extremities.

Then one day about noon Demetrios came unheralded into Melicent's resplendent prison. Through an aisle of painted pillars he came to her, striding with unwonted quickness, glittering as he moved. His robe this day was scarlet, the colour he chiefly affected. Gold glowed upon his forehead, gold dangled from his ears, and about his throat was a broad collar of gold and rubies. At his side was a cross-handled sword, in a scabbard of blue leather, curiously ornamented.

"Give thanks, my wife," Demetrios said, "that you are beautiful. For beauty was ever the spur of valour." Then quickly, joyously, he told her of how a fleet equipped by the King of Cyprus had been despatched against the province of Demetrios, and of how among the invaders were Perion of the Forest and his Free Companions. "Ey, yes, my porter has returned. I ride instantly for the coast to greet him with appropriate welcome. I pray heaven it is no sluggard or weakling that is come out against me."

Proudly Melicent replied:

"There comes against you a champion of noted deeds, a courteous and hardy gentleman, pre-eminent at swordplay. There was never any man more ready than Perion to break a lance or shatter a shield, or more eager to succour the helpless and put to shame all cowards and traitors."

Demetrios dryly said:

"I do not question that the virtues of my porter are innumerable. Therefore we will not attempt to catalogue them. Now Ahasuerus reports that even before you came to tempt me with your paltry emeralds you once held the life of Perion in your hands?" Demetrios unfastened his sword. He grasped the hand of Melicent, and laid it upon the scabbard. "And what do you hold now, my wife? You hold the death of Perion. I take the antithesis to be neat."

She answered nothing. Her seeming indifference angered him. Demetrios wrenched the sword from its scabbard, with a hard violence that made Melicent recoil. He showed the blade all covered with graved symbols of which she could make nothing.

"This is Flamberge," said the proconsul; "the weapon which was the pride and bane of my father, famed Miramon Lluagor, because it was the sword which Galas made, in the old time's heyday, for unconquerable Charlemaigne. Clerks declare it is a magic weapon and that the man who wields it is always unconquerable. I do not know. I think it is as difficult to believe in sorcery as it is to be entirely sure that all we know is not the sorcery of a drunken wizard. I very potently believe, however, that with this sword I shall kill Perion."

Melicent had plenty of patience, but astonishingly little, it seemed, for this sort of speech. "I think that you talk foolishly, seignior. And, other matters apart, it is manifest that you yourself concede Perion to be the better swordsman, since you require to be abetted by sorcery before you dare to face him."

"So, so!" Demetrios said, in a sort of grinding whisper, "you think that I am not the equal of this long-legged fellow! You would think otherwise if I had him here. You will think otherwise when I have killed him with my naked hands. Oh, very soon you will think otherwise."

He snarled, rage choking him, flung the sword at her feet and quitted her without any leave-taking. He had ridden three miles from Nacumera before he began to laugh. He perceived that Melicent at least respected sorcery, and had tricked him out of Flamberge by playing upon his tetchy vanity. Her adroitness pleased him.

Demetrios did not laugh when he found the Christian fleet had been ingloriously repulsed at sea by the Emir of Arsuf, and had never effected a landing. Demetrios picked a quarrel with the victorious admiral and killed the marplot in a public duel, but that was inadequate comfort.

"However," the proconsul reassured himself, "if my wife reports at all truthfully as to this Perion's nature it is certain that this Perion will come again." Then Demetrios went into the sacred grove upon the hillsides south of Quesiton and made an offering of myrtle-branches, rose-leaves and incense to Aphrodite of Colias.

10.
How Demetrios Wooed

AHASUERUS came and went at will. Nothing was known concerning this soft-treading furtive man except by the proconsul, who had no confidants. By his decree Ahasuerus was an honoured guest at Nacumera. And always the Jew's eyes when Melicent was near him were as expressionless as the eyes of a snake, which do not ever change.

Once she told Demetrios that she feared Ahasuerus.

"But I do not fear him, Melicent, though I have larger reason. For I alone of all men living know the truth concerning this same Jew. Therefore, it amuses me to think that he, who served my wizard father in a very different fashion, is to-day my factor and ciphers over my accounts."

Demetrios laughed, and had the Jew summoned.

This was in the Women's Garden, where the proconsul sat with Melicent in a little domed pavilion of stone-work which was gilded with red gold and crowned with a cupola of alabaster. Its pavement was of transparent glass, under which were clear running waters wherein swam red and yellow fish.

Demetrios said:

"It appears that you are a formidable person, Ahasuerus. My wife here fears you."

"Splendour of the Age," returned Ahasuerus, quietly, "it is notorious that women have long hair and short wits. There is no need to fear a Jew. The Jew, I take it, was created in order that children might evince their playfulness by stoning him, the honest show their common-sense by robbing him, and the religious display their piety by burning him. Who forbids it?"

"Ey, but my wife is a Christian and in consequence worships a Jew." Demetrios reflected. His dark eyes twinkled. "What is your opinion concerning this other Jew, Ahasuerus?"

"I know that He was the Messiah, Lord."

"And yet you do not worship Him."

The Jew said:

"It was not altogether worship He desired. He

asked that men should love Him. He does not ask love of me."

"I find that an obscure saying," Demetrios considered.

"It is a true saying, King of Kings. In time it will be made plain. That time is not yet come. I used to pray it would come soon. Now I do not pray any longer. I only wait."

Demetrios tugged at his chin, his eyes narrowed, meditating. He laughed.

Demetrios said:

"It is no affair of mine. What am I that I am called upon to have prejudices concerning the universe? It is highly probable there are gods of some sort or another, but I do not so far flatter myself as to consider that any possible god would be at all interested in my opinion of him. In any event, I am Demetrios. Let the worst come, and in whatever baleful underworld I find myself imprisoned I shall maintain myself there in a manner not unworthy of Demetrios." The proconsul shrugged at this point. "I do not find you amusing, Ahasuerus. You may go."

"I hear, and I obey," the Jew replied. He went away patiently.

Then Demetrios turned toward Melicent, rejoicing that his chattel had golden hair and was comely beyond comparison with all other women he had ever seen.

Said Demetrios:

"I love you, Melicent, and you do not love me. Do not be offended because my speech is harsh, for even though I know my candour is distasteful I must speak the truth. You have been obdurate too long, denying Kypris what is due to her. I think that your brain is giddy because of too much exulting in the magnificence of your body and in the number of men who have desired it to their own hurt. I concede your beauty, yet what will it matter a hundred years from now?

"I admit that my refrain is old. But it will presently take on a more poignant meaning, because a hundred years from now you—even you, dear Melicent!—and all the loveliness which now causes me to estimate life as a light matter in comparison with your love, will be only a bone or two. Your lustrous eyes, which are now more beautiful than it is possible to express, will be unsavoury holes and a worm will crawl through them; and what will it matter a hundred years from now?

"A hundred years from now should anyone

break open our gilded tomb, he will find Melicent to be no more admirable than Demetrios. One skull is like another, and is as lightly split with a mattock. You will be as ugly as I, and nobody will be thinking of your eyes and hair. Hail, rain and dew will drench us both impartially when I lie at your side, as I intend to do, for a hundred years and yet another hundred years. You need not frown, for what will it matter a hundred years from now?

"Melicent, I offer love and a life that derides the folly of all other manners of living; and even if you deny me, what will it matter a hundred years from now?"

His face was contorted, his speech had fervent bitterness, for even while he wooed this woman the man internally was raging over his own infatuation.

And Melicent answered:

"There can be no question of love between us, seignior. You purchased my body. My body is at your disposal under God's will."

Demetrios sneered, his ardours cooled. He said, "I have already told you, my girl, I do not care for that which can be purchased."

In such fashion Melicent abode among these

odious persons as a lily which is rooted in mire. She was a prisoner always, and when Demetrios came to Nacumera—which fell about irregularly, for now arose much fighting between the Christians and the pagans—a gem which he uncased, admired, curtly exulted in, and then, jeering at those hot wishes in his heart, locked up untouched when he went back to warfare.

To her the man was uniformly kind, if with a sort of sneer she could not understand; and he pillaged an infinity of Genoese and Venetian ships—which were notoriously the richliest laden—of jewels, veils, silks, furs, embroideries and figured stuffs, wherewith to enhance the comeliness of Melicent. It seemed an all-engulfing madness with this despot daily to aggravate his fierce desire of her, to nurture his obsession, so that he might glory in the consciousness of treading down no puny adversary.

Pride spurred him on as witches ride their dupes to a foreknown destruction. "Let us have patience," he would say.

Meanwhile his other wives peered from screened alcoves at these two and duly hated Melicent. "Let us have patience!" they said, also, but with a meaning that was more sinister.

PART THREE

DEMETRIOS

Of how Dame Melicent's fond lovers go
As comrades, working each his fellow's woe:
Each hath unhorsed the other of the twain,
And knoweth that nowhither 'twixt Ukraine
And Ormus roameth any lion's son
More eager in the hunt than Perion,
Nor any viper's sire more venomous
Through jealous hurt than is Demetrios.

II.

How Time Sped with Perion

IT is a tale which they narrate in Poictesme, telling of what befell Perion de la Forêt after he had been ransomed out of heathenry. They tell how he took service with the King of Cyprus. And the tale tells how the King of Cyprus was defeated at sea by the Emir of Arsuf; and how Perion came unhurt from that battle, and by land relieved the garrison at Japhe, and was ennobled therefor; and was afterward called the Comte de la Forêt.

Then the King of Cyprus made peace with heathendom, and Perion left him. Now Perion's skill in warfare was leased to whatsoever lord would dare contend against Demetrios and the proconsul's magic sword Flamberge: and Perion of the Forest did not inordinately concern himself as to the merits of any quarrel because of which battalions died, so long as he fought toward Melicent. Demetrios was pleased, and thrilled with the heroic joy of an athlete who finds that he unwittingly has grappled with his equal.

So the duel between these two dragged on with varying fortunes, and the years passed, and neither duellist had conquered as yet. Then King Theodoret, third of that name to rule, and once (as you have heard) a wooer of Dame Melicent, declared a crusade; and Perion went to him at Lacre Kai. It was in making this journey, they say, that Perion passed through Pseudopolis, and had speech there with Queen Helen, the delight of gods and men: and Perion conceded this Queen was well-enough to look at.

"She reminds me, indeed, of that Dame Melicent whom I serve in this world, and trust to serve in Paradise," said Perion. "But Dame Melicent has a mole on her left cheek."

"That is a pity," said an attendant lord. "A mole disfigures a pretty woman."

"I was speaking, messire, of Dame Melicent."

"Even so," the lord replied, "a mole is a blemish."

"I cannot permit these observations," said Perion. So they fought, and Perion killed his opponent, and left Pseudopolis that afternoon.

Such was Perion's way.

He came unhurt to King Theodoret, who at once

recognised in the famous Comte de la Forêt the former Vicomte de Puysange, but gave no sign of such recognition.

"Heaven chooses its own instruments," the pious King reflected: "and this swaggering Comte de la Forêt, who affects so many names, has also the name of being a warrior without any peer in Christendom. Let us first conquer this infamous proconsul, this adversary of our Redeemer, and then we shall see. It may be that heaven will then permit me to detect this Comte de la Forêt in some particularly abominable heresy. For this long-legged ruffian looks like a schismatic, and would singularly grace a rack."

So King Theodoret kissed Perion upon both cheeks, and created him generalissimo of King Theodoret's forces. It was upon St. George's day that Perion set sail with thirty-four ships of great dimensions and admirable swiftness.

"Do you bring me back Demetrios in chains," said the King, fondling Perion at parting, "and all that I have is yours."

"I mean to bring back my stolen wife, Dame Melicent," was Perion's reply: "and if I can manage it I shall also bring you this Demetrios, in return for lending me these ships and soldiers."

"Do you think," the King asked, peevishly, "that monarchs nowadays fit out armaments to replevin a woman who is no longer young, and who was always stupid?"

"I cannot permit these observations—" said Perion.

Theodoret hastily explained that his was merely a general observation, without any personal bearing.

12.
How Demetrios Was Taken

THUS it was that war awoke and raged about the province of Demetrios as tirelessly as waves lapped at its shores.

Then, after many ups and downs of carnage,[1] Perion surprised the galley of Demetrios while the proconsul slept at anchor in his own harbour of Quesiton. Demetrios fought nakedly against accoutred soldiers and had killed two of them with his hands before he could be quieted by an admiring Perion.

Demetrios by Perion's order was furnished with a sword of ordinary attributes, and Perion ridded himself of all defensive armour. The two met like an encounter of tempests, and in the outcome Demetrios was wounded so that he lay insensible.

[1] Nicolas de Caen gives here a minute account of the military and naval evolutions, with a fullness that verges upon prolixity. It appears expedient to omit all this.

Demetrios was taken as a prisoner toward the domains of King Theodoret.

"Only you are my private capture," said Perion; "conquered by my own hand and in fair fight. Now I am unwilling to insult the most valiant warrior whom I have known by valuing him too cheaply, and I accordingly fix your ransom as the person of Dame Melicent."

Demetrios bit his nails.

"Needs must," he said at last. "It is unnecessary to inform you that when my property is taken from me I shall endeavour to regain it. I shall, before the year is out, lay waste whatever kingdom it is that harbours you. Meanwhile I warn you it is necessary to be speedy in this ransoming. My other wives abhor the Frankish woman who has supplanted them in my esteem. My son Orestes, who succeeds me, will be guided by his mother. Callistion has thrice endeavoured to kill Melicent. If any harm befalls me, Callistion to all intent will reign in Nacumera, and she will not be satisfied with mere assassination. I cannot guess what torment Callistion will devise, but it will be no child's play—"

"Hah, infamy!" cried Perion. He had learned long ago how cunning the heathen were in such cruelties, and so he shuddered.

Demetrios was silent. He, too, was frightened, because this despot knew—and none knew better—that in his lordly house far oversea Callistion would find equipment for a hundred curious tortures.

"It has been difficult for me to tell you this," Demetrios then said, "because it savours of an appeal to spare me. I think you will have gleaned, however, from our former encounters, that I am not unreasonably afraid of death. Also I think that you love Melicent. For the rest, there is no person in Nacumera so untutored as to cross my least desire until my death is triply proven. Accordingly, I who am Demetrios am willing to entreat an oath that you will not permit Theodoret to kill me."

"I swear by God and all the laws of Rome—" cried Perion.

"Ey, but I am not very popular in Rome," Demetrios interrupted. "I would prefer that you swore by your love for Melicent. I would prefer an oath which both of us may understand, and I know of none other."

So Perion swore as Demetrios requested, and set about the conveyance of Demetrios into King Theodoret's realm.

13.
How They Praised Melicent

THE conqueror and the conquered sat together upon the prow of Perion's ship. It was a warm, clear night, so brilliant that the stars were invisible. Perion sighed. Demetrios inquired the reason.

Perion said:

"It is the memory of a fair and noble lady, Messire Demetrios, that causes me to heave a sigh from my inmost heart. I cannot forget that loveliness which had no parallel. Pardieu, her eyes were amethysts, her lips were red as the berries of a holly-tree. Her hair blazed in the light, bright as the sunflower glows; her skin was whiter than milk; the down of a fledgling bird was not more grateful to the touch than were her hands. There was never any person more delightful to gaze upon, and whosoever beheld her forthwith desired to render love and service to Dame Melicent."

Demetrios gave his customary lazy shrug. Demetrios said:

"She is still a brightly-coloured creature, moves gracefully, has a sweet, drowsy voice, and is as soft to the touch as rabbit's fur. Therefore, it is imperative that one of us must cut the other's throat. The deduction is perfectly logical. Yet I do not know that my love for her is any greater than my hatred. I rage against her patient tolerance of me, and I am often tempted to disfigure, mutilate, even to destroy this colourful, stupid woman, who makes me wofully ridiculous in my own eyes. I shall be happier when death has taken the woman who ventures to deal in this fashion with Demetrios."

Said Perion:

"When I first saw Dame Melicent the sea was languid, as if outworn by vain endeavours to rival the purple of her eyes. Sea-birds were adrift in the air, very close to her, and their movements were less graceful than hers. She was attired in a robe of white silk, and about her wrists were heavy bands of silver. A tiny wind played truant in order to caress her unplaited hair, because the wind was more hardy than I, and dared to love her. I did not think of love, I thought only of the noble deeds I might have done and had not done. I thought of my unworthiness, and it seemed to me that my soul writhed like an eel in sunlight, a naked, despicable thing, that was unworthy to render any love and service to Dame Melicent."

Demetrios said:

"When I first saw the girl she knew herself entrapped, her body mine, her life dependent on my whim. She waved aside such petty inconveniences, bade them await an hour when she had leisure to consider them, because nothing else was of any importance so long as my porter went in chains. I was an obstacle to her plans and nothing more; a pebble in her shoe would have perturbed her about as much as I did. Here at last, I thought, is genuine common-sense—a clear-headed decision as to your actual desire, apart from man-taught ethics, and fearless purchase of your desire at any cost. There is something not unakin to me, I reflected, in the girl who ventures to deal in this fashion with Demetrios."

Said Perion:

"Since she permits me to serve her, I may not serve unworthily. To-morrow I shall set new armies afield. To-morrow it will delight me to see their tents rise in your meadows, Messire Demetrios, and to see our followers meet in clashing combat, by hundreds and thousands, so mightily that men will sing of it when we are gone. To-morrow one of us must kill the other. To-night we drink our wine in amity. I have not time to hate you, I have not time to like or dislike any living person, I must devote all faculties that heaven gave me to the love and service of Dame Melicent."

Demetrios said:

"To-night we babble to the stars and dream vain dreams as other fools have done before us. To-morrow rests—perhaps—with heaven; but, depend upon it, Messire de la Forêt, whatever we may do to-morrow will be foolishly performed, because we are both besotted by bright eyes and lips and hair. I trust to find our antics laughable. Yet there is that in me which is murderous when I reflect that you and she do not dislike me. It is the distasteful truth that neither of you considers me to be worth the trouble. I find such conduct irritating, because no other persons have ever ventured to deal in this fashion with Demetrios."

"Demetrios, already your antics are laughable, for you pass blindly by the revelation of heaven's splendour in heaven's masterwork; you ignore the miracle; and so do you find only the stings of the flesh where I find joy in rendering love and service to Dame Melicent."

"Perion, it is you that play the fool, in not recognising that heaven is inaccessible and doubtful. But clearer eyes perceive the not at all doubtful dullness of wit, and the gratifying accessibility of every woman when properly handled,—yes, even of her who dares to deal in this fashion with Demetrios."

Thus they would sit together, nightly, upon the prow of Perion's ship and speak against each other in the manner of a Tenson, as these two rhapsodised of Melicent until the stars grew lustreless before the sun.

14.
How Perion Braved Theodoret

THE city of Megaris (then Theodoret's capital) was ablaze with bonfires on the night that the Comte de la Forêt entered it at the head of his forces. Demetrios, meanly clothed, his hands tied behind him, trudged sullenly beside his conqueror's horse. Yet of the two the gloomier face showed below the count's coronet, for Perion did not relish the impendent interview with King Theodoret. They came thus amid much shouting to the Hôtel d'Ebelin, their assigned quarters, and slept there.

Next morning, about the hour of prime, two men-at-arms accompanied a fettered Demetrios into the presence of King Theodoret. Perion of the Forest preceded them. He pardonably swaggered, in spite of his underlying uneasiness, for this last feat, as he could not ignore, was a performance which Christendom united to applaud.

They came thus into a spacious chamber, very inadequately lighted. The walls were unhewn stone. There was but one window, of uncoloured glass; and it was guarded by iron bars. The floor was bare of rushes. On one side was a bed with tattered hangings of green, which were adorned with rampant lions worked in silver thread much tarnished; to the right hand stood a *prie-dieu.* Between these isolated articles of furniture, and behind an unpainted table sat, in a high-backed chair, a wizen and shabbily-clad old man. This was Theodoret, most pious and penurious of monarchs. In attendance upon him were Fra Battista, prior of the Grey Monks, and Melicent's near kinsman, once the Bishop, now the Cardinal, de Montors, who, as was widely known, was the actual monarch of this realm. The latter was smartly habited as a cavalier and showed in nothing like a churchman.

The infirm King arose and came to meet the champion who had performed what many generals of Christendom had vainly striven to achieve. He embraced the conqueror of Demetrios as one does an equal.

Said Theodoret:

"Hail, my fair friend! you who have lopped the right arm of heathenry! To-day, I know, the saints hold festival in heaven. I cannot recompense you, since God alone is omnipotent. Yet ask now what you will, short of my crown, and it is yours." The old man kissed the chief of all his treasures, a bit of the True Cross, which hung upon his breast supported by a chain of gold.

"The King has spoken," Perion returned. "I ask the life of Demetrios."

Theodoret recoiled, like a small flame which is fluttered by its kindler's breath. He cackled thinly, saying:

"A jest or so is privileged in this high hour. Yet we ought not to make a jest of matters which concern the Church. Am I not right, Ayrart? Oh, no, this merciless Demetrios is assuredly that very Antichrist whose coming was foretold. I must relinquish him to Mother Church, in order that he may be equitably tried, and be baptised—since even he may have a soul—and afterward be burned in the market-place."

"The King has spoken," Perion replied. "I too have spoken."

There was a pause of horror upon the part of King Theodoret. He was at first in a mere whirl. Theodoret said:

"You ask, in earnest, for the life of this Demetrios, this arch-foe of our Redeemer, this spawn of Satan, who has sacked more of my towns than I have fingers on this wasted hand! Now, now that God has singularly favoured me—!" Theodoret snarled and gibbered like a frenzied ape, and had no longer the ability to articulate.

"Beau sire, I fought the man because he infamously held Dame Melicent, whom I serve in this world without any reservation, and trust to serve in Paradise. His person, and this alone, will ransom Melicent."

"You plan to loose this fiend!" the old King cried. "To stir up all this butchery again!"

"Sire, pray recall how long I have loved Melicent. Reflect that if you slay Demetrios, Dame Melicent will be left destitute in heathenry. Remember that she will be murdered through the hatred of this man's other wives whom her inestimable beauty has supplanted." Thus Perion entreated.

All this while the cardinal and the proconsul had been appraising each other. It was as though they two had been the only persons in the dimly-lit apartment. They had not met before. "Here is my match," thought each of these two; "here, if the world affords it, is my peer in cunning and bravery."

And each lusted for a contest, and with something of mutual comprehension.

In consequence they stinted pity for Theodoret, who unfeignedly believed that whether he kept or broke his recent oath damnation was inevitable. "You have been ill-advised—" he stammered. "I do not dare release Demetrios— My soul would answer that enormity— But it was sworn upon the Cross— Oh, ruin either way! Come now, my gallant captain," the King barked. "I have gold, lands, and jewels—"

"Beau sire, I have loved this my dearest lady since the time when both of us were little more than children, and each day of the year my love for her has been doubled. What would it avail me to live in however lofty estate when I cannot daily see the treasure of my life?"

Now the Cardinal de Montors interrupted, and his voice was to the ear as silk is to the fingers.

"Beau sire," said Ayrart de Montors, "I speak in all appropriate respect. But you have sworn an oath which no man living may presume to violate."

"Oh, true, Ayrart!" the fluttered King assented. "This blusterer holds me as in a vise." He turned to Perion again, fierce, tense and fragile, like an angered cat. "Choose now! I will make you the wealthiest person in my realm— My son, I warn you that since Adam's time women have been the devil's peculiar bait. See now, I am not angry. Heh, I remember, too, how beautiful she was. I was once tempted much as you are tempted. So I pardon you. I will give you my daughter Ermengarde in marriage, I will make you my heir, I will give you half my kingdom—" His voice rose, quavering; and it died now, for he foreread the damnation of Theodoret's soul while he fawned before this impassive Perion.

"Since Love has taken up his abode within my heart," said Perion, "there has not ever been a vacancy therein for any other thought. How may I help it if Love recompenses my hospitality by afflicting me with a desire which can neither subdue the world nor be subdued by it?"

Theodoret continued like the rustle of dead leaves:

"—Else I must keep my oath. In that event you may depart with this unbeliever. I will accord you twenty-four hours wherein to accomplish this. But, oh, if I lay hands upon either of you within the twenty-fifth hour I will not kill my prisoner at once. For first I must devise unheard-of torments—"

The King's face was not agreeable to look upon.

Yet Perion encountered it with an untroubled gaze until Battista spoke, saying:

"I promise worse. The Book will be cast down, the bells be tolled, and all the candles snuffed—ah, very soon!" Battista licked his lips, gingerly, just as a cat does.

Then Perion was moved, since excommunication is more terrible than death to any of the Church's loyal children, and he was now more frightened than the King. And so Perion thought of Melicent a while before he spoke.

Said Perion:

"I choose. I choose hell fire in place of riches and honour, and I demand the freedom of Demetrios."

"Go!" the King said. "Go hence, blasphemer. Hah, you will weep for this in hell. I pray that I may hear you then, and laugh as I do now—"

He went away, and was followed by Battista, who whispered of a makeshift. The cardinal remained and saw to it that the chains were taken from Demetrios.

"In consequence of Messire de la Forêt's—as I must term it—most unchristian decision," said the cardinal, "it is not impossible, Messire the Proconsul, that I may head the next assault upon your territory—"

Demetrios laughed. He said:

"I dare to promise your Eminence that reception you would most enjoy."

"I had hoped for as much," the cardinal returned; and he too laughed. To do him justice, he did not know of Battista's makeshift.

The cardinal remained when they had gone. Seated in a king's chair, Ayrart de Montors meditated rather wistfully upon that old time when he, also, had loved Melicent whole-heartedly. It seemed a great while ago, made him aware of his maturity.

He had put love out of his life, in common with all other weaknesses which might conceivably hinder the advancement of Ayrart de Montors. In consequence, he had climbed far. He was not dissatisfied. It was a man's business to make his way in the world, and he had done this.

"My cousin is a brave girl, though," he said aloud, "I must certainly do what I can to effect her rescue as soon as it is convenient to send another expedition against Demetrios."

Then the cardinal set about concoction of a moving sonnet in praise of Monna Vittoria de' Pazzi. Desperation loaned him extraordinary eloquence (as he complacently reflected) in addressing this obdurate woman, who had held out against his lovemaking for six weeks now.

15.

How Perion Fought

DEMETRIOS and Perion, by the quick turn of fortune previously recorded, were allied against all Christendom. They got arms at the Hôtel d'Ebelin, and they rode out of the city of Megaris, where the bonfires lighted over-night in Perion's honour were still smouldering, amid loud execrations. Fra Battista had not delayed to spread the news of King Theodoret's dilemma. The burghers yelled menaces; but, knowing that an endeavour to constrain the passage of these champions would prove unwholesome for at least a dozen of the arrestors, they cannily confined their malice to a vocal demonstration.

Demetrios rode unhelmeted, intending that these snarling little people of Megaris should plainly see the man whom they most feared and hated.

It was Perion who spoke first. They had passed the city walls, and had mounted the hill which leads toward the Forest of Sannazaro. Their road lay through a rocky pass above which the leaves of spring were like sparse traceries on a blue cupola, for April had not come as yet.

"I meant," said Perion, "to hold you as the ransom of Dame Melicent. I fear that is impossible. I, who am a landless man, have neither servitors nor any castle wherein to retain you as a prisoner. I earnestly desire to kill you, forthwith, in single combat; but when your son Orestes knows that you are dead he will, so you report, kill Melicent. And yet it may be you are lying."

Perion was of a tall imperious person, and accustomed to command. He had black hair, grey eyes which challenged you, and a thin pleasant face which was not pleasant now.

"You know that I am not a coward—" Demetrios began.

"Indeed," said Perion, "I believe you to be the hardiest warrior in the world."

"Therefore I may without dishonour repeat to you that my death involves the death of Melicent. Orestes hates her for his mother's sake. I think, now we have fought so often, that each of us knows I do not fear death. I grant I had Flamberge to wield, a magic weapon—" Demetrios shook himself, like a dog coming from the water, for to consider an extraneous invincibility was nauseous. "However! I who am Demetrios protest I will not fight with you, that I will accept any insult rather than risk my life in any quarrel extant, because I know the moment that Orestes has made certain I am no longer to be feared he will take vengeance on Dame Melicent."

"Prove this!" said Perion, and with deliberation he struck Demetrios. Full in the face he struck the swart proconsul, and in the ensuing silence you could hear a feeble breeze that strayed about the tree-tops, but you could hear nothing else. And Perion, strong man, the willing scourge of heathendom, had half a mind to weep.

Demetrios had not moved a finger. It was appalling. The proconsul's countenance had throughout the hue of wood-ashes, but his fixed eyes were like blown embers.

"I believe that it is proved," said Demetrios, "since both of us are still alive." He whispered this.

"In fact the thing is settled," Perion agreed. "I know that nothing save your love for Melicent could possibly induce you to decline a proffered battle. When Demetrios enacts the poltroon I am the most hasty of all men living to assert that the excellency of his reason is indisputable. Let us get on! I have only five hundred sequins, but this will be enough to buy your passage back to Quesiton. And inasmuch as we are near the coast—"

"I think some others mean to have a spoon in that broth," Demetrios returned. "For look, messire!"

Perion saw that far beneath them a company of retainers in white and purple were spurring up the hill. "It is Duke Sigurd's livery," said Perion.

Demetrios forthwith interpreted and was amused by their common ruin. He said, grinning:

"Pious Theodoret has sworn a truce of twenty-four hours, and in consequence might not send any of his own lackeys after us. But there was nothing to prevent the dropping of a hint into the ear of his brother in-law, because you servitors of Christ excel in these distinctions."

"This is hardly an opportunity for theological debate," Perion considered. "And for the rest, time presses. It is your instant business to escape." He gave his tiny bag of gold to his chief enemy. "Make for Narenta. It is a free city and unfriendly to Theodoret. If I survive I will come presently and fight with you for Melicent."

"I shall do nothing of the sort," Demetrios

equably returned. "Am I the person to permit the man whom I most hate—you who have struck me and yet live!—to fight alone against some twenty adversaries! Oh, no, I shall remain, since after all, there are only twenty."

"I was mistaken in you," Perion replied, "for I had thought you loved Dame Melicent as I do. I find too late that you would estimate your private honour as set against her welfare."

The two men looked upon each other. Long and long they looked, and the heart of each was elated. "I comprehend," Demetrios said. He clapped spurs to his horse and fled as a coward would have fled. This was one occasion in his life when he overcame his pride, and should in consequence be noted.

The heart of Perion was glad.

"Oh, but at times," said Perion, "I wish that I might honourably love this infamous and lustful pagan."

Afterward Perion wheeled and met Duke Sigurd's men. Then like a reaper cutting a field of wheat Sire Perion showed the sun his sword and went about his work, not without harvesting.

In that narrow way nothing could be heard but the striking of blows on armour and the clash of swords which bit at one another. The Comte de la

Forêt, for once, allowed himself the privilege of fighting in anger. He went without a word toward this hopeless encounter, as a drunkard to his bottle. First Perion killed Ruggiero of the Lamberti and after that Perion raged as a wolf harrying sheep. Six other stalwart men he cut down, like a dumb maniac among tapestries. His horse was slain and lay blocking the road, making a barrier behind which Perion fought. Then Perion encountered Giacomo di Forio, and while the two contended Gulio the Red very warily cast his sword like a spear so that it penetrated Perion's left shoulder and drew much blood. This hampered the lone champion. Marzio threw a stone which struck on Perion's crest and broke the fastenings of Perion's helmet. Instantly Giacomo gave him three wounds, and Perion stumbled, the sunlight glossing his hair. He fell and they took him. They robbed the corpses of their surcoats, which they tore in strips. They made ropes of this bloodied finery, and with these ropes they bound Perion of the Forest, whom twenty men had conquered at last.

He laughed feebly, like a person bedrugged; but in the midst of this superfluous defiance Perion swooned because of many injuries. He knew that with fair luck Demetrios had a sufficient start. The heart of Perion exulted, thinking that Melicent was saved.

It was the happier for him he was not ever destined to comprehend the standards of Demetrios.

16.

How Demetrios Meditated

DEMETRIOS came without any hindrance into Narenta, a free city. He believed his Emperor must have sent galleys toward Christendom to get tidings of his generalissimo, but in this city of merchants Demetrios heard no report of them. Yet in the harbour he found a trading-ship prepared for traffic in the country of the pagans; the sail was naked to the wind, the anchor-chain was already shortened at the bow. Demetrios bargained with the captain of this vessel, and in the outcome paid him four hundred sequins. In exchange the man agreed to touch at the Needle of Ansignano that afternoon and take Demetrios aboard. Since the proconsul had no passport, he could not with safety endeavour to elude those officers of the Tribunal who must endorse the ship's passage at Piaja.

Thus about sunset Demetrios waited the ship's

coming, alone upon the Needle. This promontory is like a Titan's finger of black rock thrust out into the water. The day was perishing, and the querulous sea before Demetrios was an unresting welter of gold and blood.

He thought of how he had won safely through a horde of dangers, and the gross man chuckled. He considered that unquestioned rulership of every person near Demetrios which awaited him oversea, and chiefly he thought of Melicent whom he loved even better than he did the power to sneer at everything the world contained. And the proconsul chuckled.

He said, aloud:

"I owe very much to Messire de la Forêt. I owe far more than I can estimate. For, by this, those lackeys will have slain Messire de la Forêt or else they will have taken Messire de la Forêt to King Theodoret, who will piously make an end of this handsome idiot. Either way, I shall enjoy tranquillity and shall possess my Melicent until I die. Decidedly, I owe a deal to this self-satisfied tall fool."

Thus he contended with his irritation. It may be that the man was never sane; it is certain that the mainspring of his least action was an inordinate pride. Now hatred quickened, spreading from a flicker of distaste; and his faculties were stupefied, as though he faced a girdling conflagration. It was not possible to hate adequately this Perion who had struck Demetrios of Anatolia and perhaps was not yet dead; nor could Demetrios think of any sufficing requital for this Perion who dared to be so tall and handsome and young-looking when Demetrios was none of these things, for this Perion whom Melicent had loved and loved to-day. And Demetrios of Anatolia had fought with a charmed sword against a person such as this, safe as an angler matched against a minnow; Demetrios of Anatolia, now at the last, accepted alms from what had been until to-day a pertinacious gnat. Demetrios was physically shaken by disgust at the situation, and in the sunset's glare his swarthy countenance showed like that of Belial among the damned.

"The life of Melicent hangs on my safe return to Nacumera. . . . Ey, what is that to me!" the proconsul cried aloud. "The thought of Melicent is sweeter than the thought of any god. It is not sweet enough to bribe me into living as this Perion's debtor."

So when the ship touched at the Needle, a half-hour later, that spur of rock was vacant. Demetrios had untethered his horse, had thrown away his sword and other armour, and had torn his garments; afterward he rolled in the first puddle he discovered. Thus he set out afoot, in grimy rags—for no one marks a beggar upon the highway—and thus he came again into the realm of King Theodoret, where certainly nobody looked for Demetrios to come unarmed.

With the advantage of a quiet advent, as was quickly proven, he found no check for a notorious leave-taking.

17.
How a Minstrel Came

DEMETRIOS came to Megaris where Perion lay fettered in the Castle of San' Alessandro, then a new building. Perion's trial, condemnation, and so on, had consumed the better part of an hour, on account of the drunkenness of one of the Inquisitors, who had vexatiously impeded these formalities by singing love-songs; but in the end it had been salutarily arranged that the Comte de la Forêt be torn apart by four horses upon the St. Richard's day ensuing.

Demetrios, having gleaned this knowledge in a pothouse, purchased a stout file, a scarlet cap and a lute. Ambrogio Bracciolini, head-gaoler at the fortress—so the gossips told Demetrios—had been a jongleur in youth, and minstrels were always welcome guests at San' Alessandro.

The gaoler was a very fat man with icy little

eyes. Demetrios took his measure to a hair's breadth as this Bracciolini straddled in the doorway.

Demetrios had assumed an admirable air of simplicity.

"God give you joy, messire," he said, with a simper; "I come bringing a precious balsam which cures all sorts of ills, and heals the troubles both of body and mind. For what is better than to have a pleasant companion to sing and tell merry tales, songs and facetious histories?"

"You appear to be something of a fool," Bracciolini considered, "but all do not sleep who snore. Come, tell me what are your accomplishments."

"I can play the lute, the violin, the flageolet, the harp, the syrinx and the regals," the other replied; "also the Spanish penola that is struck with a quill, the organistrum that a wheel turns round, the wait so delightful, the rebeck so enchanting, the little gigue that chirps up on high, and the great horn that booms like thunder."

Bracciolini said:

"That is something. But can you throw knives into the air and catch them without cutting your fingers? Can you balance chairs and do tricks with string? or imitate the cries of birds? or throw a somersault and walk on your head? Ha, I thought not. The Gay Science is dying out, and young practitioners neglect these subtile points. It was not so in my day. However, you may come in."

So when night fell Demetrios and Bracciolini sat snug and sang of love, of joy, and arms. The fire burned bright, and the floor was well covered with gaily tinted mats. White wines and red were on the table.

Presently they turned to canzons of a more indecorous nature. Demetrios sang the loves of Douzi and Ishtar, which the gaoler found remarkable. He said so and crossed himself. "Man, man, you must have been afishing in the mid-pit of hell to net such filth."

"I learned that song in Nacumera," said Demetrios, "when I was a prisoner there with Messire de la Forêt. It was a favourite song with him."

"Ay?" said Bracciolini. He looked at Demetrios very hard, and Bracciolini pursed his lips as if to whistle. The gaoler scented from afar a bribe, but the face of Demetrios was all vacant cheerfulness.

Bracciolini said, idly:

"So you served under him? I remember that he was taken by the heathen. A woman ransomed him, they say."

Demetrios, able to tell a tale against any man,

told now the tale of Melicent's immolation, speaking with vivacity and truthfulness in all points save that he represented himself to have been one of the ransomed Free Companions.

Bracciolini's careful epilogue was that the proconsul had acted foolishly in not keeping the emeralds.

"He gave his enemy a weapon against him," Bracciolini said, and waited.

"Oh, but that weapon was never used. Sire Perion found service at once under King Bernart, you will remember. Therefore Sire Perion hid away these emeralds against future need—under an oak in Sannazaro, he told me. I suppose they lie there yet."

"Humph!" said Bracciolini. He for a while was silent. Demetrios sat adjusting the strings of the lute, not looking at him.

Bracciolini said, "There were eighteen of them, you tell me? and all fine stones?"

"Ey?—oh, the emeralds? Yes, they were flawless, messire. The smallest was larger than a robin's egg. But I recall another song we learned at Nacumera—"

Demetrios sang the loves of Lucius and Fotis.

Bracciolini grunted, "Admirable" in an abstracted fashion, muttered something about the duties of his office, and left the room. Demetrios heard him lock the door outside and waited stolidly.

Presently Bracciolini returned in full armour, a naked sword in his hand.

"My man,"—and his voice rasped—"I believe you to be a rogue. I believe that you are contriving the escape of this infamous Comte de la Forêt. I believe you are attempting to bribe me into conniving at his escape. I shall do nothing of the sort, because, in the first place, it would be an abominable violation of my oath of office, and in the second place, it would result in my being hanged."

"Messire, I swear to you—!" Demetrios cried, in excellently feigned perturbation.

"And in addition, I believe you have lied to me throughout. I do not believe you ever saw this Comte de la Forêt. I very certainly do not believe you are a friend of this Comte de la Forêt's, because in that event you would never have been mad enough to admit it. The statement is enough to hang you twice over. In short, the only thing I can be certain of is that you are out of your wits."

"They say that I am moonstruck," Demetrios

answered; "but I will tell you a secret. There is a wisdom lies beyond the moon, and it is because of this that the stars are glad and admirable."

"That appears to me to be nonsense," the gaoler commented; and he went on: "Now I am going to confront you with Messire de la Forêt. If your story prove to be false, it will be the worse for you."

"It is a true tale. But sensible men close the door to him who always speaks the truth."

"These reflections are not to the purpose," Bracciolini submitted, and continued his argument: "In that event Messire de la Forêt will undoubtedly be moved by your fidelity in having sought out him whom all the rest of the world has forsaken. You will remember that this same fidelity has touched me to such an extent that I am granting you an interview with your former master. Messire de la Forêt will naturally reflect that a man once torn in four pieces has no particular use for emeralds. He will, I repeat, be moved. In his emotion, in his gratitude, in mere decency, he will reveal to you the location of those eighteen stones, all flawless. If he should not evince a sufficiency of such appropriate and laudable feeling, I tell you candidly, it will be the worse for you. And now get on!"

Bracciolini pointed the way and Demetrios cringed

through the door. Bracciolini followed with drawn sword. The corridors were deserted. The head-gaoler had seen to that.

His position was simple. Armed, he was certainly not afraid of any combination between a weaponless man and a fettered one. If this jongleur had lied, Bracciolini meant to kill him for his insolence. Bracciolini's own haphazard youth had taught him that a jongleur had no civil rights, was a creature to be beaten, robbed, or stabbed with impunity.

Upon the other hand, if the vagabond's tale were true, one of two things would happen. Either Perion would not be brought to tell where the emeralds were hidden, in which event Bracciolini would kill the jongleur for his bungling; or else the prisoner would tell everything necessary, in which event Bracciolini would kill the jongleur for knowing more than was convenient. This Bracciolini had an honest respect for gems and considered them to be equally misplaced when under an oak or in a vagabond's wallet.

Consideration of such avarice may well have heartened Demetrios when the well-armoured gaoler knelt in order to unlock the door of Perion's cell. As an asp leaps, the big and supple hands of the proconsul gripped Bracciolini's neck from behind, and silenced speech.

Demetrios, who was not tall, lifted the gaoler as high as possible, lest the beating of armoured feet upon the slabs disturb any of the other keepers, and Demetrios strangled his dupe painstakingly. The keys, as Demetrios reflected, were luckily attached to the belt of this writhing thing, and in consequence had not jangled on the floor. It was an inaudible affair and consumed in all some ten minutes. Then with the sword of Bracciolini Demetrios cut Bracciolini's throat. In such matters Demetrios was thorough.

18.

How They Cried Quits

DEMETRIOS went into Perion's cell and filed away the chains of Perion of the Forest. Demetrios thrust the gaoler's corpse under the bed, and washed away all stains before the door of the cell, so that no awkward traces might remain. Demetrios locked the door of an unoccupied apartment and grinned as Old Legion must have done when Judas fell.

More thanks to Bracciolini's precautions, these two got safely from the confines of San' Alessandro, and afterward from the city of Megaris. They trudged on a familiar road. Perion would have spoken, but Demetrios growled, "Not now, messire." They came by night to that pass in Sannazaro which Perion had held against a score of men-at-arms.

Demetrios turned. Moonlight illuminated the

warriors' faces and showed the face of Demetrios as sly and leering. It was less the countenance of a proud lord than a carved head on some old waterspout.

"Messire de la Forêt," Demetrios said, "now we cry quits. Here our ways part till one of us has killed the other, as one of us must surely do."

You saw that Perion was tremulous with fury. "You knave," he said, "because of your pride you have imperilled your accursed life—your life on which the life of Melicent depends! You must need delay and rescue me, while your spawn inflicted hideous infamies on Melicent! Oh, I had never hated you until to-night!"

Demetrios was pleased.

"Behold the increment," he said, "of the turned cheek and of the contriving of good for him that had despitefully used me! Be satisfied, O young and zealous servitor of Love and Christ. I am alone, unarmed and penniless, among a people whom I have never been at pains even to despise. Presently I shall be taken by this vermin, and afterward I shall be burned alive. Theodoret is quite resolved to make of me a candle which will light his way to heaven."

"That is true," said Perion; "and I cannot permit that you be killed by anyone save me, as soon as I can afford to kill you."

The two men talked together, leagued against entire Christendom. Demetrios had thirty sequins and Perion no money at all. Then Perion showed the ring which Melicent had given him, as a love-token, long ago, when she was young and ignorant of misery. He valued it as he did nothing else.

Perion said:

"Oh, very dear to me is this dear ring which once touched a finger of that dear young Melicent whom you know nothing of! Its gold is my lost youth, the gems of it are the tears she has shed because of me. Kiss it, Messire Demetrios, as I do now for the last time. It is a favour you have earned."

Then these two went as mendicants—for no one marks a beggar upon the highway—into Narenta, and they sold this ring, in order that Demetrios might be conveyed oversea, and that the life of Melicent might be preserved. They found another vessel which was about to venture into heathendom. Their gold was given to the captain; and, in exchange, the bargain ran, his ship would touch at

Assignano, a little after the ensuing dawn, and take Demetrios aboard.

Thus the two lovers of Melicent foreplanned the future, and did not admit into their accounting vagarious Dame Chance.

19.
How Flamberge Was Lost

THESE hunted men spent the following night upon the Needle, since there it was not possible for an adversary to surprise them. Perion's was the earlier watch, until midnight, and during this time Demetrios slept. Then the proconsul took his equitable turn. When Perion awakened the hour was after dawn.

What Perion noted first, and within thirty feet of him, was a tall galley with blue and yellow sails. He perceived that the promontory was thronged with heathen sailors, who were unlading the ship of various bales and chests. Demetrios, now in the costume of his native country, stood among them giving orders. And it seemed, too, to Perion, in the moment of waking, that Dame Mélusine, whom Perion had loved so long ago, also stood among them; yet, now that Perion rose and faced Demetrios, she was not visible anywhere, and Perion wondered dimly over his wild dream that she had been there at all. But more importunate matters were in hand.

The proconsul grinned malevolently.

"This is a ship that once was mine," he said. "Do you not find it droll that Euthyclos here should have loved me sufficiently to hazard his life in order to come in search of me? Personally, I consider it preposterous. For the rest, you slept so soundly, Messire de la Forêt, that I was unwilling to waken you. Then, too, such was the advice of a person who has some influence with the water-folk, people say, and who was perhaps the means of bringing this ship hither so opportunely. I do not know. She is gone now, you see, intent as always on her own ends. Well, well! her ways are not our ways, and it is wiser not to meddle with them."

But Perion, unarmed and thus surrounded, understood only that he was lost.

"Messire Demetrios," said Perion, "I never thought to ask a favour of you. I ask it now. For the ring's sake, give me at least a knife, Messire Demetrios. Let me die fighting."

"Why, but who spoke of fighting? For the ring's sake, I have caused the ship to be rifled of what valuables they had aboard. It is not much, but it is all I have. And you are to accept my apologies for the somewhat miscellaneous nature of the cargo, Messire de la Forêt—consisting, as it does, of armours and gems, camphor and ambergris, carpets of raw silk, teakwood and precious metals, rugs of Yemen leather, enamels, and I hardly know what else besides. For Euthyclos, as you will readily understand, was compelled to masquerade as a merchant-trader."

Perion shook his head, and declared:

"You offer enough to make me a wealthy man. But I would prefer a sword."

At that Demetrios grimaced, saying, "I had hoped to get off more cheaply." He unbuckled the cross-handled sword which he now wore and handed it to Perion. "This is Flamberge," Demetrios continued—"that magic blade which Galas made, in the old time's heyday, for Charlemaigne. It was with this sword that I slew my father, and this sword is as dear to me as your ring was to you. The man who wields it is reputed to be unconquerable. I do not know about that, but in any event I yield Flamberge to you as a free gift. I might have known it was the only gift you would accept." His swart face lighted. "Come presently and fight with me for Melicent. Perhaps it will amuse me to ride out to battle and know I shall not live to see the sunset. Already it seems laughable that you will probably kill me with this very sword which I am touching now."

The champions faced each other, Demetrios in a half-wistful mirth, and Perion in half-grudging pity. Long and long they looked.

Demetrios shrugged. Demetrios said:

"For such as I am, to love is dangerous. For such as I am, nor fire nor meteor hurls a mightier bolt than Aphrodite's shaft, or marks its passage by more direful ruin. But you do not know Euripides?—a fidgety-footed liar, Messire the Comte, who occasionally blunders into the clumsiest truths. Yes, he is perfectly right; all things this goddess laughingly demolishes while she essays haphazard flights about the world as unforeseeably as travels a bee. And, like the bee, she wilfully dispenses honey, and at other times a wound."

Said Perion, who was no scholar:

"I glory in our difference. For such as I am, love is sufficient proof that man was fashioned in God's image."

"Ey, there is no accounting for a taste in aphorisms," Demetrios replied. He said, "Now I embark." Yet he delayed, and spoke with unaccustomed awkwardness. "Come, you who have been generous till this! will you compel me to desert you here—quite penniless?"

Said Perion:

"I may accept a sword from you. I do accept it gladly. But I may not accept anything else."

"That would have been my answer. I am a lucky man," Demetrios said, "to have provoked an enemy so worthy of my opposition. We two have fought an honest and notable duel, wherein our weapons were not made of steel. I pray you harry me as quickly as you may; and then we will fight with swords till I am rid of you or you of me."

"Assuredly, I shall not fail you," answered Perion.

These two embraced and kissed each other. Afterward Demetrios went into his own country, and Perion remained, girt with the magic sword Flamberge. It was not all at once Perion recollected that the wearer of Flamberge is unconquerable, if ancient histories are to be believed, for in deduction Perion was leisurely.

Now on a sudden he perceived that Demetrios had flung control of the future to Perion, as one gives money to a sot, entirely prescient of how it will be used. Perion had his moment of bleak rage.

"I will not cog the dice to my advantage any more than you!" said Perion. He drew the sword of Charlemaigne and brandished it and cast it as far as even strong Perion could cast, and the sea swallowed it. "Now God alone is arbiter!" cried Perion, "and I am not afraid."

He stood a pauper and a friendless man. Beside his thigh hung a sorcerer's scabbard of blue leather, curiously ornamented, but it was emptied of power. Yet Perion laughed exultingly, because he was elate with dreams of the future. And for the rest, he was aware it is less grateful to remember plaudits than to recall the exercise of that in us which is not merely human.

20.

How Perion Got Aid

THEN Perion turned from the Needle of Assignano, and went westward into the Forest of Columbiers. He had no plan. He wandered in the high woods that had never yet been felled or ordered, as a beast does in watchful care of hunters.

He came presently to a glade which the sunlight flooded without obstruction. There was in this place a fountain, which oozed from under an iron-coloured boulder incrusted with grey lichens and green moss. Upon the rock a woman sat, her chin propped by one hand, and she appeared to consider remote and pleasant happenings. She was clothed throughout in white, with metal bands about her neck and arms; and her loosened hair, which was coloured like straw, and was as pale as the hair of children, glittered about her, and shone frostily where it lay outspread upon the rock behind her.

She turned toward Perion without any haste or surprise, and Perion saw that this woman was Dame Mélusine, whom he had loved to his own hurt (as you have heard) when Perion served King Helmas. She did not speak for a long while, but she lazily considered Perion's honest face in a sort of whimsical regret for the adoration she no longer found there.

"Then it was really you," he said, in wonder, "whom I saw talking with Demetrios when I awakened to-day."

"You may be sure," she answered, "that my talking was in no way injurious to you. Ah, no, had I been elsewhere, Perion, I think you would by this have been in Paradise." Then Mélusine fell again to meditation. "And so you do not any longer either love or hate me, Perion?" Here was an odd echo of the complaint Demetrios had made.

"That I once loved you is a truth which neither of us, I think, may ever quite forget," said Perion, very quiet. "I alone know how utterly I loved you —no, it was not I who loved you, but a boy that is dead now. King's daughter, all of stone, O cruel woman and hateful, O sleek, smiling traitress! today no man remembers how utterly I loved you, for the years are as a mist between the heart of the dead boy and me, so that I may no longer see the boy's heart clearly. Yes, I have forgotten much. . . . Yet even to-day there is that in me which is faithful to you, and I cannot give you the hatred which your treachery has earned."

Mélusine spoke shrewdly. She had a sweet, shrill voice.

"But I loved you, Perion—oh, yes, in part I loved you, just as one cannot help but love a large and faithful mastiff. But you were tedious, you annoyed me by your egotism. Yes, my friend, you think too much of what you owe to Perion's honour; you are perpetually squaring accounts with heaven, and you are too intent on keeping the balance in your favour to make a satisfactory lover." You saw that Mélusine was smiling in the shadow of her pale hair. "And yet you are very droll when you are unhappy," she stated ambiguously.

He replied:

"I am, as heaven made me, a being of mingled nature. So I remember without distaste old happenings which now seem scarcely credible. I cannot quite believe that it was you and I who were so happy when youth was common to us. . . . O Mélusine, I have almost forgotten that if the world were searched between the sunrise and the sunsetting the Mélusine I loved would not be found. I only know that a woman has usurped the voice of Mélusine, and that this woman's eyes also are blue, and that this woman smiles as Mélusine was used to smile when I was young. I walk with ghosts, king's daughter, and I am none the happier."

"Ay, Perion," she wisely answered, "for the spring is at hand, intent upon an ageless magic. I am no less comely than I was, and my heart, I think, is tenderer. You are yet young, and you are very beautiful, my brave mastiff. . . . And neither of us is moved at all! For us the spring is only a dotard sorcerer who has forgotten the spells of yesterday. I think that it is pitiable, although I would not have it otherwise." She waited, fairy-like and wanton, seeming to premeditate a delicate mischief.

He declared, sighing, "No, I would not have it otherwise."

Then presently Mélusine arose. She said:

"You are a hunted man, unarmed—oh, yes, I know. Demetrios talked freely, because the son of Miramon Lluagor has good and ancient reasons to trust me. Besides, it was not for nothing that Pressina was my mother, and I know many things, pilfering light from the past to shed it upon the future. Come now with me to Brunbelois. I am too deeply in your debt, my Perion. For the sake of that boy who is dead—as you tell me—you may honourably accept of me a horse, arms, and a purse, because I loved that boy after my fashion."

"I take your bounty gladly," he replied; and he added conscientiously: "I consider that I am not at liberty to refuse of anybody any honest means of serving my lady Melicent."

Mélusine parted her lips as if about to speak, and then seemed to think better of it. It is probable she was already informed concerning Melicent; she certainly asked no questions. Mélusine only shrugged, and laughed afterward, and the man and the woman turned toward Brunbelois. At times a shaft of sunlight would fall on her pale hair and convert it into silver, as these two went through the high woods that had never yet been felled or ordered.

PART FOUR

AHASUERUS

Of how a knave hath late compassion
On Melicent's forlorn condition;
For which he saith as ye shall after hear:
"Dame, since that game we play costeth too dear,
My truth I plight, I shall you no more grieve
By my behest, and here I take my leave
As of the fairest, truest and best wife
That ever yet I knew in all my life."

21.

How Demetrios Held His Chattel

IT is a tale which they narrate in Poictesme, telling how Demetrios returned into the country of the pagans and found all matters there as he had left them. They relate how Melicent was summoned.

And the tale tells how upon the stairway by which you descended from the Women's Garden to the citadel—people called it the Queen's Stairway, because it was builded by Queen Rudabeh very long ago when the Emperor Zal held Nacumera—Demetrios waited with a naked sword. Below were four of his soldiers, picked warriors. This stairway was of white marble, and a sphinx carved in green porphyry guarded each balustrade.

"Now that we have our audience," Demetrios said, "come, let the games begin."

One of the soldiers spoke. It was that Euthyclos

who (as you have heard) had ventured into Christendom at the hazard of his life to rescue the proconsul. Euthyclos was a man of the West Provinces and had followed the fortunes of Demetrios since boyhood.

"King of the Age," cried Euthyclos, "it is grim hearing that we must fight with you. But since your will is our will, we must endure this testing, although we find it bitter as aloes and hot as coals. Dear lord and master, none has put food to his lips for whose sake we would harm you willingly, and we shall weep to-night when your ghost passes over and through us."

Demetrios answered:

"Rise up and leave this idleness! It is I that will clip the ends of my hair to-night for the love of you, my stalwart knaves. Such weeping as is done your wounds will perform."

At that they addressed themselves to battle, and Melicent perceived she was witnessing no child's play. The soldiers had attacked in unison, and before the onslaught Demetrios stepped lightly back. But his sword flashed as he moved, and with a grunt Demetrios, leaning far forward, dug deep into the throat of his foremost assailant. The sword penetrated and caught in a link of the gold chain about the fellow's neck, so that Demetrios was forced to wrench the weapon free, twisting it, as the dying man stumbled backward. Prostrate, the soldier did not cry out, but only writhed and gave a curious bubbling noise as his soul passed.

"Come," Demetrios said, "come now, you others, and see what you can win of me. I warn you it will be dearly purchased."

And Melicent turned away, hiding her eyes. She was obscurely conscious that a wanton butchery went on, hearing its blows and groans as if from a great distance, while she entreated the Virgin for deliverance from this foul place.

Then a hand fell upon Melicent's shoulder, rousing her. It was Demetrios. He breathed quickly, but his voice was gentle.

"It is enough," he said. "I shall not greatly need Flamberge when I encounter that ruddy innocent who is so dear to you."

He broke off. Then he spoke again, half jeering, half wistful. Said Demetrios:

"I had hoped that you would look on and admire my cunning at swordplay. I was anxious to seem admirable somehow in your eyes. . . . I failed. I know very well that I shall always fail. I know that Nacumera will fall, that some day in your native land people will say, 'That aged woman yonder was once the wife of Demetrios of Anatolia, who was pre-eminent among the heathen.' Then they will tell of how I cleft the head of an Emperor who had likened me to Priapos, and how I dragged his successor from behind an arras where he hid from me, to set him upon the throne I did not care to take; and they will tell how for a while great fortune went with me, and I ruled over much land, and was dreaded upon the wide sea, and raised the battlecry in cities that were not my own, fearing nobody. But you will not think of these matters, you will think only of your children's ailments, of baking and sewing and weaving tapestries, and of directing little household tasks. And the spider will spin her web in my helmet, which will hang as a trophy in the hall of Messire de la Forêt."

Then he walked beside her into the Women's Garden, keeping silence for a while. He seemed to deliberate, to reach a decision. All at once Demetrios began to tell of that magnanimous contest which he had fought out in Theodoret's country with Perion of the Forest.

"To do the long-legged fellow simple justice," said the proconsul, as epilogue, "there is no hardier knight alive. I shall always wonder whether or no I would have spared him had the water-demon's daughter not intervened in his behalf. Yes, I have had some previous dealings with her. Perhaps the less said concerning them, the better." Demetrios reflected for a while, rather sadly; then his swart face cleared. "Give thanks, my wife, that I have found an enemy who is not unworthy of me. He will come soon, I think, and then we will fight to the death. I hunger for that day."

All praise of Perion, however worded, was as wine to Melicent. Demetrios saw as much, noted how the colour in her cheeks augmented delicately, how her eyes grew kindlier. It was his cue. Thereafter Demetrios very often spoke of Perion in that locked palace where no echo of the outer world might penetrate except at the proconsul's will. He told Melicent, in an unfeigned admiration, of Perion's courage and activity, declaring that no other captain since the days of those famous generals, Hannibal and Joshua, could lay claim to such preeminence in general estimation; and Demetrios narrated how the Free Companions had ridden through many kingdoms at adventure, serving many lords with valour and always fighting applaudably. To talk of Perion delighted Melicent: it was with such bribes that Demetrios purchased where his riches did not avail; and Melicent no longer avoided him.

There is scope here for compassion. The man's love, if it be possible so to call that force which mastered him, had come to be an incessant malady. It poisoned everything, caused him to find his statecraft tedious, his power profitless, and his vices gloomy. But chief of all he fretted over the standards by which the lives of Melicent and Perion were guided. Demetrios thought these criteria comely, he had discovered them to be unshakable, and he despairingly knew that as long as he trusted in the judgment heaven gave him they must always appear to him supremely idiotic. To bring Melicent to his own level or to bring himself to hers was equally impossible. There were moments when he hated her.

Thus the months passed, and the happenings of another year were chronicled; and as yet neither Perion nor Ayrart de Montors came to Nacumera, and the long plain before the citadel stayed tenantless save for the jackals crying there at night.

"I wonder that my enemies do not come," Demetrios said. "It cannot be they have forgotten you and me. That is impossible." He frowned and sent spies into Christendom.

22.
How Misery Held Nacumera

THEN one day Demetrios came to Melicent, and he was in a surly rage.

"Rogues all!" he grumbled. "Oh, I am wasted in this paltry age. Where are the giants and tyrants, and stalwart single-hearted champions of yesterday? Why, they are dead, and have become rotten bones. I will fight no longer. I will read legends instead, for life nowadays is no longer worthy of love or hatred."

Melicent questioned him, and he told how his spies reported that the Cardinal de Montors could now not ever head an expedition against Demetrios' territories. The Pope had died suddenly in the course of the preceding October, and it was necessary to name his successor. The College of Cardinals had reached no decision after three days' balloting. Then, as is notorious, Dame Mélusine, as always hand in glove with Ayrart de Montors, held conference with the bishop who inspected the cardinals' dinner before it was carried into the apartments where these prelates were imprisoned together until, in edifying seclusion from all worldly influences, they should have prayerfully selected the next Pope.

The Cardinal of Genoa received on the fourth day a chicken stuffed with a deed to the palaces of Monticello and Soriano; the Cardinal of Parma a similarly dressed fowl which made him master of the bishop's residence at Porto with its furniture and wine-cellar; while the Cardinals Orsino, Savelli, St. Angelo and Colonna were served with food of the same ingratiating sort. Such nourishment cured them of indecision, and Ayrart de Montors had presently ascended the papal throne under the title of Adrian VII, servant to the servants of God. His days of military captaincy were over.

Demetrios deplored the loss of a formidable adversary, and jeered at the fact that the vicarship of heaven had been settled by six hens. But he particularly fretted over other news his spies had brought, which was the information that Perion had wedded Dame Mélusine, and had begotten two lusty children—Bertram and a daughter called Blaniferte—and now enjoyed the opulence and sovereignty of Brunbelois.

Demetrios told this unwillingly. He turned away his eyes in speaking, and doggedly affected to rearrange a cushion, so that he might not see the face of Melicent. She noted his action and was grateful.

Demetrios said, bitterly:

"It is an old and tawdry history. He has forgotten you, Melicent, as a wise man will always put aside the dreams of his youth. To Cynara the Fates accord but a few years; a wanton Lyce laughs, cheats her adorers, and outlives the crow. There is an unintended moral here—" Demetrios said, "Yet you do not forget."

"I know nothing as to this Perion you tell me of. I only know the Perion I loved has not forgotten," answered Melicent.

And Demetrios, evincing a twinge like that of gout, demanded her reasons. It was a May morning, very hot and still, and Demetrios sat with his Christian wife in the Court of Stars.

Said Melicent:

"It is not unlikely that the Perion men know today has forgotten me and the service which I joyed to render Perion. Let him who would understand the mystery of the Crucifixion first become a lover! I pray for old sake's sake that Perion and his lady may taste of every prosperity. Indeed, I do not envy her. Rather I pity her, because last night I wandered through a certain forest hand-in-hand with a young Perion, whose excellencies she will never know as I know them in our own woods."

Said Demetrios, "Do you console yourself with dreams?" The swart man grinned.

Melicent said:

"Now it is always twilight in these woods, and the light there is neither green nor gold, but both colours intermingled. It is like a friendly cloak for all who have been unhappy, even very long ago. Iseult is there, and Thisbe, too, and many others, and they are not severed from their lovers now. . . . Sometimes Dame Venus passes, riding upon a panther, and low-hanging leaves clutch at her tender flesh. Then Perion and I peep from a coppice, and are very glad and a little frightened in the heart of our own woods."

Said Demetrios, "Do you console yourself with madness?" He showed no sign of mirth.

Melicent said:

"Ah, no, the Perion whom Mélusine possesses is

but a man—a very happy man, I pray of God and all His saints. I am the luckier, who may not ever lose the Perion that to-day is mine alone. And though I may not ever touch this younger Perion's hands—and their palms were as hard as leather in that dear time now overpast—or see again his honest and courageous face, the most beautiful among all the faces of men and women I have ever seen, I do not grieve immeasurably, for nightly we walk hand-in-hand in our own woods."

Demetrios said, "Ay; and then night passes, and dawn comes to light my face, which is the most hideous to you among all the faces of men and women!"

But Melicent said only:

"Seignior, although the severing daylight endures for a long while, I must be brave and worthy of Perion's love—nay, rather, of the love he gave me once. I may not grieve so long as no one else dares enter into our own woods."

"Now go," cried the proconsul, when she had done, and he had noted her soft, deep, devoted gaze at one who was not there; "now go before I slay you!" And this new Demetrios whom she then saw was featured like a devil in sore torment.

Wonderingly Melicent obeyed him.

Thought Melicent, who was too proud to show her anguish:

"I could have borne aught else, but this I am too cowardly to bear without complaint. I am a very contemptible person. I ought to love this Mélusine, who no doubt loves her husband quite as much as I love him—how could a woman do less?—and yet I cannot love her. I can only weep that I, robbed of all joy, and with no children to bewail me, must travel very tediously toward death, a friendless person cursed by fate, while this Mélusine laughs with her children. She has two children, as Demetrios reports. I think the boy must be the more like Perion. I think she must be very happy when she lifts that boy into her lap."

Thus Melicent; and her full-blooded husband was not much more light-hearted. He went away from Nacumera shortly, in a shaking rage which robbed him of his hands' control, intent to kill and pillage, and, in fine, to make all other persons share his misery.

23.
How Demetrios Cried Farewell

AND then one day, when the proconsul had been absent some six weeks, Ahasuerus fetched Dame Melicent into the Court of Stars. Demetrios lay upon the divan supported by many pillows, as though he had not ever stirred since that first day when an unfettered Melicent, who was a princess then, exulted in her youth and comeliness.

"Stand there," he said, and did not move at all, "that I may see my purchase."

And presently he smiled, though wryly. Demetrios said next:

"Of my own will I purchased misery. Yea, and death also. It is amusing. . . . Two days ago, in a brief skirmish, a league north of Calonak, the Frankish leader met me hand to hand. He has endeavoured to do this for a long while. I also wished it. Nothing could be sweeter than to feel the horse beneath me wading in his blood, I thought. . . . Ey, well, he dismounted me at the first encounter, though I am no weakling. I cannot understand quite how it happened. Pious people will say some deity was offended, but, for my part, I think my horse stumbled. It does not seem to matter now. What really matters, more or less, is that it would appear the man broke my backbone as one snaps a straw, since I cannot move a limb of me."

"Seignior," said Melicent, "you mean that you are dying!"

He answered, "Yes; but it is a trivial discomfort, now I see that it grieves you a little."

She spoke his name some three times, sobbing. It was in her mind even then how strange the happening was that she should grieve for Demetrios.

"O Melicent," he harshly said, "let us have done with lies! That Frankish captain who has brought about my death is Perion de la Forêt. He has not ever faltered in the duel between us since your paltry emeralds paid for his first armament.—Why, yes, I lied. I always hoped the man would do as in his place I would have done. I hoped in vain. For many long and hard-fought years this handsome maniac has been assailing Nacumera, tirelessly. Then the water-demon's daughter, that strange and wayward woman of Brunbelois, attempted to ensnare him. And that too was in vain. She failed, my spies reported—even Dame Mélusine, who had not ever failed before in such endeavours."

"But certainly the foul witch failed!" cried Melicent. A glorious change had come into her face, and she continued, quite untruthfully, "Nor did I ever believe that this vile woman had made Perion prove faithless."

"No, the fool's lunacy is rock, like yours. *En cor gentil domnei per mort no passa,* as they sing in your native country. . . . Ey, how indomitably I lied, what pains I took, lest you should ever know of this! And now it does not seem to matter any more. . . . The love this man bears for you," snarled Demetrios, "is sprung of the High God whom we diversely worship. The love I bear you is human, since I, too, am only human." And Demetrios chuckled. "Talk, and talk, and talk! There is no bird in any last year's nest."

She laid her hand upon his unmoved hand, and found it cold and swollen. She wept to see the broken tyrant, who to her at least had been not all unkind.

He said, with a great hunger in his eyes:

"So likewise ends the duel which was fought between us two. I would salute the victor if I could. . . . Ey, Melicent, I still consider you and Perion are fools. We have a not intolerable world to live in, and common-sense demands we make the most of every tidbit this world affords. Yet you can find in it only an exercising-ground for infatuation, and in all its contents—pleasures and pains alike—only so many obstacles for rapt insanity to override. I do not understand this mania; I would I might have known it, none the less. Always I envied you more than I loved you. Always my desire was less to win the love of Melicent than to love Melicent as Melicent loved Perion. I was incapable of this. Yet I have loved you. That was the reason, I believe, I put aside my purchased toy." It seemed to puzzle him.

"Fair friend, it is the most honourable of reasons. You have done chivalrously. In this, at least, you have done that which would be not unworthy of Perion de la Forêt." A woman never avid for strained subtleties, it may be that she never understood, quite, why Demetrios laughed.

He said:

"I mean to serve you now, as I had always meant to serve you some day. Ey, yes, I think I always meant to give you back to Perion as a free gift. Meanwhile to see, and to writhe in seeing your perfection, has meant so much to me that daily I have delayed such a transfiguration of myself until to-morrow." The man grimaced. "My son Orestes, who will presently succeed me, has been summoned. I will order that he conduct you at once into Perion's camp—yonder by Quesiton. I think I shall not live three days."

"I would not leave you, friend, until—"

His grin was commentary and completion equally. Demetrios observed:

"A dead dog has no teeth wherewith to serve even virtue. Oh, no, my women hate you far too greatly. You must go straightway to this Perion, while Demetrios of Anatolia is alive, or else not ever go."

She had no words. She wept, and less for joy of winning home to Perion at last than for her grief that Demetrios was dying. Woman-like, she could remember only that the man had loved her in his fashion. And, woman-like, she could but wonder at the strength of Perion.

Then Demetrios said:

"I must depart into a doubtful exile. I have been powerful and valiant, I have laughed loud, I have drunk deep, but heaven no longer wishes Demetrios to exist. I am unable to support my sadness, so near am I to my departure from all I have loved. I cry farewell to all diversions and sports, to well-fought battles, to furred robes of vair and of silk, to noisy merriment, to music, to vain-gloriously coloured gems, and to brave deeds in open sunlight; for I desire—and I entreat of every person—only compassion and pardon.

"Chiefly I grieve because I must leave Melicent behind me, unfriended in a perilous land, and abandoned, it may be, to the malice of those who wish her ill. I was a noted warrior, I was mighty of muscle, and I could have defended her stoutly. But I lie broken in the hand of Destiny. It is necessary I depart into the place where sinners, whether crowned or ragged, must seek for unearned mercy. I cry farewell to all that I have loved, to all that I have injured; and so in chief to you, dear Melicent, I cry farewell, and of you in chief I crave compassion and pardon.

"O eyes and hair and lips of Melicent, that I have loved so long, I do not hunger for you now. Yet, as a dying man, I cry to the clean soul of Melicent—the only adversary that in all my lifetime I who was once Demetrios could never conquer. A ravening beast was I, and as a beast I raged to see you so unlike me. And now, a dying beast, I cry to you, but not for love, since that is overpast. I cry for pity that I have not earned, for pardon which I have not merited. Conquered and impotent, I cry to you, O soul of Melicent, for compassion and pardon.

"Melicent, it may be that when I am dead, when nothing remains of Demetrios except his tomb, you will comprehend I loved, even while I hated, what is divine in you. Then since you are a woman, you will lift your lover's face between your hands, as you have never lifted my face, Melicent, and you will tell him of my folly merrily; yet since you are a woman, you will sigh afterward, and you will not deny me compassion and pardon."

She gave him both—she who was prodigal of charity. Orestes came, with Ahasuerus at his heels, and Demetrios sent Melicent into the Women's Garden, so that father and son might talk together. She waited in this place for a half-hour, just as the proconsul had commanded her, obeying him for the last time. It was strange to think of that.

It was not gladness which Melicent knew for a brief while. Rather, it was a strange new comprehension of the world. To Melicent the world seemed very lovely.

Indeed, the Women's Garden on this morning lacked nothing to delight each sense. Its hedges were of flowering jessamine; its walkways were spread with new sawdust tinged with crocus and vermilion and with mica beaten into a powder; and the place was rich in fruit-bearing trees and welling waters. The sun shone, and birds chaunted merrily to the right hand and to the left. Dog-headed apes, sacred to the moon, were chattering in the trees. There was a statue in this place, carved out of black stone, in the likeness of a woman, having enamelled eyes and three rows of breasts, with the lower part of her body confined in a sheath; and upon the glistening pedestal of this statue chameleons sunned themselves with distended throats. Round about Melicent were nodding armaments of roses and gillyflowers and narcissi and amaranths, and many violets and white lilies, and other flowers of all kinds and colours.

To Melicent the world seemed very lovely. Here was a world created by Eternal Love that people might serve love in it not all unworthily. Here were anguishes to be endured, and time and human frailty and temporal hardship—all for love to mock at; a sea or two for love to sever, a man-made law or so for love to override, a shallow wisdom for love to deny, in exultance that these ills at most were only corporal hindrances. This done, you have earned the right to come—come hand-in-hand —to heaven whose liege-lord was Eternal Love.

Thus Melicent, who knew that Perion loved her.

She sat on a stone bench. She combed her golden hair, not heeding the more coarse gray hairs which here and there were apparent nowadays. A peacock came and watched her with bright, hard, small eyes; and he craned his glistening neck this way and that way, as though he were wondering at this other shining and gaily coloured creature, who seemed so happy.

She did not dare to think of seeing Perion again. Instead, she made because of him a little song, which had not any words, so that it is not possible here to retail this song.

Thus Melicent, who knew that Perion loved her.

24.
How Orestes Ruled

MELICENT returned into the Court of Stars; and as she entered, Orestes lifted one of the red cushions from Demetrios' face. The eyes of Ahasuerus, who stood by negligently, were as expressionless as the eyes of a snake.

"The great proconsul laid an inconvenient mandate upon me," said Orestes. "The great proconsul has been removed from us in order that his splendour may enhance the glories of Elysium."

She saw that the young man had smothered his own father in the flesh as Demetrios lay helpless; and knew thereby that Orestes was indeed the son of Demetrios.

"Go," this Orestes said thereafter; "go, and remember I am master here."

Said Melicent, "And by which door?" A little hope there was as yet.

But he, as half in shame, had pointed to the entrance of the Women's Garden. "I have no enmity against you, outlander. Yet my mother desires to talk with you. Also there is some bargaining to be completed with Ahasuerus here."

Then Melicent knew what had prompted the proconsul's murder. It seemed unfair Callistion should hate her with such bitterness; yet Melicent remembered certain thoughts concerning Dame Mélusine, and did not wonder at Callistion's mania half so much as did Callistion's son.

"I must endure discomfort and, it may be, torture for a little longer," said Melicent, and laughed whole-heartedly. "Oh, but to-day I find a cure for every ill," said Melicent; and thereupon she left Orestes as a princess should.

But first she knelt by that which yesterday had been her master.

"I have no word of praise or blame to give you in farewell. You were not admirable, Demetrios. But you depart upon a fearful journey, and in my heart there is just memory of the long years wherein according to your fashion you were kind to me. A bargain is a bargain. I sold with open eyes that which you purchased. I may not reproach you."

Then Melicent lifted the dead face between her

hands, as mothers caress their boys in questioning them.

"I would I had done this when you were living," said Melicent, "because I understand now that you loved me in your fashion. And I pray that you may know I am the happiest woman in the world, because I think this knowledge would now gladden you. I go to slavery, Demetrios, where I was queen, I go to hardship, and it may be that I go to death. But I have learned this assuredly—that love endures, that the strong knot which unites my heart and Perion's heart can never be untied. Oh, living is a higher thing than you or I had dreamed! And I have in my heart just pity, poor Demetrios, for you who never found the love of which I must endeavour to be worthy. A curse was I to you unwillingly, as you—I now believe—have been to me against your will. So at the last I turn anew to bargaining, and cry—in your deaf ears—*Pardon for pardon, O Demetrios!*"

Then Melicent kissed pitiable lips which would not ever sneer again, and, rising, passed into the Women's Garden, proudly and unafraid.

Ahasuerus shrugged so patiently that she was half afraid. Then, as a cloud passes, she saw that all further buffetings would of necessity be trivial.

For Perion, as she now knew, was very near to her—single of purpose, clean of hands, and filled with such a love as thrilled her with delicious fears of her own poor unworthiness.

25.
How Women Talked Together

DAME MELICENT walked proudly through the Women's Garden, and presently entered a grove of orange trees, the most of which were at this season about their flowering. In this place was an artificial pool by which the trees were nourished. On its embankment sprawled the body of young Diophantus, a child of some ten years of age, Demetrios' son by Tryphera. Orestes had strangled Diophantus in order that there might be no rival to Orestes' claims. The lad lay on his back, and his left arm hung elbow-deep in the water, which swayed it gently.

Callistion sat beside the corpse and stroked its limp right hand. She had hated the boy throughout his brief and merry life. She thought now of his likeness to Demetrios.

She raised toward Melicent the dilated eyes of

one who has just come from a dark place. Callistion said:

"And so Demetrios is dead. I thought I would be glad when I said that. Hah, it is strange I am not glad."

She rose, as though with hard effort, as a decrepit person might have done. You saw that she was dressed in a long gown of black, pleated to the knees, having no clasp or girdle, and bare of any ornamentation except a gold star on each breast.

Callistion said:

"Now, through my son, I reign in Nacumera. There is no person who dares disobey me. Therefore, come close to me that I may see the beauty which besotted this Demetrios, whom, I think now, I must have loved."

"Oh, gaze your fill," said Melicent, "and know that had you possessed a tithe of my beauty you might have held the heart of Demetrios." For it was in Melicent's mind to provoke the woman into killing her before worse befell.

But Callistion only studied the proud face for a long while, and knew there was no lovelier person between two seas. For time here had pillaged very sparingly; and if Dame Melicent had not any longer the first beauty of her girlhood, Callistion had nowhere seen a woman more handsome than this hated Frankish thief.

Callistion said:

"No, I was not ever so beautiful as you. Yet this Demetrios loved me when I, too, was lovely. You never saw the man in battle. I saw him, single-handed, fight with Abradas and three other knaves who stole me from my mother's home—oh, very long ago! He killed all four of them. He was like a horrible unconquerable god when he turned from that finished fight to me. He kissed me then—blood-smeared, just as he was. . . . I like to think of how he laughed and of how strong he was."

The woman turned and crouched by the dead boy, and seemed painstakingly to appraise her own reflection on the water's surface.

"It is gone now, the comeliness Demetrios was pleased to like. I would have waded Acheron—singing—rather than let his little finger ache. He knew as much. Only it seemed a trifle, because your eyes were bright and your fair skin was unwrinkled. In consequence the man is dead. Oh, Melicent, I wonder why I am so sad!"

Callistion's meditative eyes were dry, but those of Melicent were not. And Melicent came to the

Dacian woman, and put one arm about her in that dim, sweet-scented place, saying, "I never meant to wrong you."

Callistion did not seem to heed. Then Callistion said:

"See now! Do you not see the difference between us!" These two were kneeling side by side, and each looked into the water.

Callistion said:

"I do not wonder that Demetrios loved you. He loved at odd times many women. He loved the mother of this carrion here. But afterward he would come back to me, and lie asprawl at my feet with his big crafty head between my knees; and I would stroke his hair, and we would talk of the old days when we were young. He never spoke of you. I cannot pardon that."

"I know," said Melicent. Their cheeks touched now.

"There is only one master who could teach you that drear knowledge—"

"There is but one, Callistion."

"The man would be tall, I think. He would, I know, have thick, brown, curling hair—"

"He has black hair, Callistion. It glistens like a raven's wing."

"His face would be all pink and white, like yours—"

"No, tanned like yours, Callistion. Oh, he is like an eagle, very resolute. His glance bedwarfs you. I used to be afraid to look at him, even when I saw how foolishly he loved me—"

"I know," Callistion said. "All women know. Ah, we know many things—"

She reached with her free arm across the body of Diophantus and presently dropped a stone into the pool. She said:

"See how the water ripples. There is now not any reflection of my poor face or of your beauty. All is as wavering as a man's heart. . . . And now your beauty is regathering like coloured mists. Yet I have other stones."

"Oh, and the will to use them!" said Dame Melicent.

"For this bright thieving beauty is not any longer yours. It is mine now, to do with as I may elect—as yesterday it was the plaything of Demetrios. . . . Why, no! I think I shall not kill you. I have at hand three very cunning Cheylas—the men who carve and reshape children into such droll monsters. They cannot change your eyes, they tell me. That is a pity, but I can have one plucked out. Then

I shall watch my Cheylas as they widen your mouth from ear to ear, take out the cartilage from your nose, wither your hair till it will always be like rotted hay, and turn your skin—which is like velvet now—the colour of baked mud. They will as deftly strip you of that beauty which has robbed me as I pluck up this blade of grass. . . . Oh, they will make you the most hideous of living things, they assure me. Otherwise, as they agree, I shall kill them. This done, you may go freely to your lover. I fear, though, lest you may not love him as I loved Demetrios."

And Melicent said nothing.

"For all we women know, my sister, our appointed curse. To love the man, and to know the man loves just the lips and eyes Youth lends to us—oho, for such a little while! Yes, it is cruel. And therefore we are cruel—always in thought and, when occasion offers, in the deed."

And Melicent said nothing. For of that mutual love she shared with Perion, so high and splendid that it made of grief a music, and wrung a new sustainment out of every cross, as men get cordials of bitter herbs, she knew there was no comprehension here.

26.
How Men Ordered Matters

ORESTES came into the garden with Ahasuerus and nine other attendants. The master of Nacumera did not speak a syllable while his retainers seized Callistion, gagged her, and tied her hands with cords. They silently removed her. One among them bore on his shoulders the slim corpse of Diophantus, which was interred the same afternoon (with every appropriate ceremony) in company with that of his father. Orestes had the nicest sense of etiquette.

This series of swift deeds was performed with such a glib precipitancy that it was as though the action had been rehearsed a score of times. The garden was all drowsy peace now that Orestes spread his palms in a gesture of deprecation. A little distance from him, Ahasuerus with his forefinger drew upon the water's surface designs which appeared to amuse the Jew.

"She would have killed you, Melicent," Orestes said, "though all Olympos had marshalled in interdiction. That would have been irreligious. Moreover, by Hercules! I have not time to choose sides between snarling women. He who hunts with cats will catch mice. I aim more highly. And besides, by an incredible forced march, this Comte de la Forêt and all his Free Companions are battering at the gates of Nacumera—"

Hope blazed. "You know that were I harmed he would spare no one. Your troops are all at Calonak. Oh, God is very good!" said Melicent.

"I do not asperse the deities of any nation. It is unlucky. None the less, your desires outpace your reason. Grant that I had not more than fifty men to defend the garrison, yet Nacumera is impregnable except by starvation. We can sit snug a month. Meanwhile our main force is at Calonak, undoubtedly. Yet my infatuated father had already recalled these troops, in order that they might escort you into Messire de la Forêt's camp. Now I shall use these knaves quite otherwise. They will arrive within two days, and to the rear of Messire de la Forêt, who is encamped before an impregnable fortress. To the front unscalable walls, and behind him, at a moderate computation, three swords to his one. All this in a valley from which Dædalos might possibly escape, but certainly no other man. I count this Perion of the Forest as already dead."

It was a lumbering Orestes who proclaimed each step in his enchained deductions by the descent of a blunt forefinger upon the palm of his left hand. Demetrios had left a son but not an heir.

Yet the chain held. Melicent tested every link and found each obdurate. She foresaw it all. Perion would be surrounded and overpowered. "And these troops come from Calonak because of me!"

"Things fall about with an odd patness, as you say. It should teach you not to talk about divinities lightly. Also, by this Jew's advice, I mean to further the gods' indisputable work. You will appear upon the walls of Nacumera at dawn tomorrow, in such a garb as you wore in your native country when the Comte de la Forêt first saw you. Ahasuerus estimates this Perion will not readily leave pursuit of you in that event, whatever his lieutenants urge, for you are very beautiful."

Melicent cried aloud, "A bitter curse this beauty has been to me, and to all men who have desired it."

"But I do not desire it," said Orestes. "Else I would not have sold it to Ahasuerus. I desire only the governorship of some province on the frontier where I may fight daily with stalwart adversaries, and ride past the homes of conquered persons who hate me. Ahasuerus here assures me that the Emperor will not deny me such employment when I bring him the head of Messire de la Forêt. The raids of Messire de la Forêt have irreligiously annoyed our Emperor for a long while."

She muttered, "Thou that once wore a woman's body—!"

"—And I take Ahasuerus to be shrewd in all respects save one. For he desires trivialities. A wise man knows that women are the sauce and not the meat of life; Ahasuerus, therefore, is not wise. And in consequence I do not lack a handsome bribe for this Bathyllos whom our good Emperor—misguided man!—is weak enough to love; my mother goes in chains; and I shall get my province."

Here Orestes laughed. And then the master of Nacumera left Dame Melicent alone with Ahasuerus.

27.
How Ahasuerus Was Candid

WHEN Orestes had gone, the Jew remained unmoved. He continued to dabble his finger-tips in the water as one who meditates. Presently he dried them on either sleeve so that he seemed to embrace himself.

Said he, "What instruments we use at need!"

She said, "So you have purchased me, Ahasuerus?"

"Yes, for a hundred and two minæ. That is a great sum. You are not as the run of women, though. I think you are worth it."

She did not speak. The sun shone, and birds chaunted merrily to the right hand and to the left. She was considering the beauty of these gardens which seemed to sleep under a dome of hard, polished blue—the beauty of this cloistered Nacumera, wherein so many infamies writhed and contended like a nest of little serpents.

"Do you remember, Melicent, that night at Fomor Beach when you snatched a lantern from my hand? Your hand touched my hand, Melicent."

She answered, "I remember."

"I first of all saw that it was a woman who was aiding Perion to escape. I considered Perion a lucky man, for I had seen the woman's face."

She remained silent.

"I thought of this woman very often. I thought of her even more frequently after I had talked with her at Bellegarde, telling of Perion's captivity. . . . Melicent," the Jew said, "I make no songs, no protestations, no phrases. My deeds must speak for me. Concede that I have laboured tirelessly." He paused, his gaze lifted, and his lips smiled. His eyes stayed mirthless. "This mad Callistion's hate of you, and of the Demetrios who had abandoned her, was my first stepping-stone. By my advice a tiny wire was fastened very tightly around the fetlock of a certain horse, between the foot and the heel, and the hair was smoothed over this wire. Demetrios rode that horse in his last battle. It stumbled, and our terrible proconsul was thus brought to death. Callistion managed it. Thus I betrayed Demetrios."

Melicent said, "You are too foul for hell to swallow." And Ahasuerus manifested indifference to this imputed fault.

"Thus far I had gone hand-in-hand with an insane Callistion. Now our ways parted. She desired only to be avenged on you, and very crudely. That did not accord with my plan. I fell to bargaining. I purchased with—O rarity of rarities!—a little rational advice and much gold as well. Thus in due season I betrayed Callistion. Well, who forbids it?"

She said:

"God is asleep. Therefore you live, and I—alas! —must live for a while longer."

"Yes, you must live for a while longer—oh, and I, too, must live for a while longer!" the Jew returned. His voice had risen in a curious quavering wail. It was the first time Melicent ever knew him to display any emotion.

But the mood passed, and he said only:

"Who forbids it? In any event, there is a venerable adage concerning the buttering of parsnips. So I content myself with asking you to remember that I have not ever faltered. I shall not falter now. You loathe me. Who forbids it? I have known from the first that you detested me, and I have always considered your verdict to err upon the side of charity. Believe me, you will never loathe Ahasuerus as I do. And yet I coddle this poor knave sometimes—oh, as I do to-day!" he said.

And thus they parted.

28.

How Perion Saw Melicent

THE manner of the torment of Melicent was this: A little before dawn she was conducted by Ahasuerus and Orestes to the outermost turrets of Nacumera, which were now beginning to take form and colour. Very suddenly a flash of light had flooded the valley, the big crimson sun was instantaneously apparent as though he had leaped over the bleeding night-mists. Darkness and all night's adherents were annihilated. Pelicans and geese and curlews were in uproar, as at a concerted signal. A buzzard yelped thrice like a dog, and rose in a long spiral from the cliff to Melicent's right hand. He hung motionless, a speck in the clear zenith, uncannily anticipative. Warmth flooded the valley.

Now Melicent could see the long and narrow plain beneath her. It was overgrown with a tall coarse grass which, rippling in the dawn-wind, resembled moving waters from this distance, save where clumps of palm trees showed like islands. Farther off, the tents of the Free Companions were as the white, sharp teeth of a lion. Also she could see—and did not recognise—the helmet-covered head of Perion catch and reflect the sunrays dazzlingly, where he knelt in the shimmering grass just out of bowshot.

Now Perion could see a woman standing, in the new-born sunlight, under many gaily coloured banners. The maiden was attired in a robe of white silk, and about her wrists were heavy bands of silver. Her hair blazed in the light, bright as the sunflower glows; her skin was whiter than milk; the down of a fledgling bird was not more grateful to the touch than were her hands. There was never anywhere a person more delightful to gaze upon, and whosoever beheld her forthwith desired to render love and service to Dame Melicent. This much could Perion know, whose fond eyes did not really see the woman upon the battlements but, instead, young Melicent as young Perion had first beheld her walking by the sea at Bellegarde.

Thus Perion, who knelt in adoration of that listless girl, all white and silver, and gold, too, where her blown hair showed like a halo. Desirable and lovelier than words may express seemed Melicent to Perion as she stood thus in lonely exaltation, and behind her, glorious banners fluttered, and the blue sky took on a deeper colour. What Perion saw was like a church window when the sun shines through it. Ahasuerus perfectly understood the baiting of a trap.

Perion came into the open plain before the castle and called on her dear name three times. Then Perion, naked to his enemies, and at the disposal of the first pagan archer that chose to shoot him down, sang cheerily the waking-song which Melicent had heard a mimic Amphitryon make in Dame Alcmena's honour, very long ago, when people laughed and Melicent was young and ignorant of misery.

Sang Perion, *"Rei glorios, verais lums e clardatz—"* or, in other wording:

"Thou King of glory, veritable light, all-powerful deity! be pleased to succour faithfully my fair, sweet friend. The night that severed us has been long and bitter, the darkness has been shaken by bleak winds, but now the dawn is near at hand.

"My fair sweet friend, be of good heart! We have been tormented long enough by evil dreams. Be of good heart, for the dawn is approaching! The east is astir. I have seen the orient star which heralds day. I discern it clearly, for now the dawn is near at hand."

The song was no great matter; but the splendid futility of its performance amid such touch-and-go surroundings Melicent considered to be august. And consciousness of his words' poverty, as Perion thus lightly played with death in order to accord due honour to the lady he served, was to Dame Melicent in her high martyrdom as is the twist of a dagger in an already fatal wound; and made her love augment.

Sang Perion:

"My fair sweet friend, it is I, your servitor, who cry to you, *Be of good heart!* Regard the sky and the stars now growing dim, and you will see that I have been an untiring sentinel. It will presently fare the worse for those who do not recognise that the dawn is near at hand.

"My fair sweet friend, since you were taken from me I have not ever been of a divided mind. I have kept faith, I have not failed you. Hourly I have entreated God and the Son of Mary to have compassion upon our evil dreams. And now the dawn is near at hand."

"My poor, bruised, puzzled boy," thought Melicent, as she had done so long ago, "how came you to be blundering about this miry world of ours? And how may I be worthy?"

Orestes spoke. His voice disturbed the woman's rapture thinly, like the speech of a ghost, and she remembered now that a bustling world was her antagonist.

"Assuredly," Orestes said, "this man is insane. I will forthwith command my archers to despatch him in the middle of his caterwauling. For at this distance they cannot miss him."

But Ahasuerus said:

"No, seignior, not by my advice. If you slay this Perion of the Forest, his retainers will speedily abandon a desperate siege and retreat to the coast. But they will never retreat so long as the man lives and sways them, and we hold Melicent, for, as you plainly see, this abominable reprobate is quite besotted with love of her. His death would win you praise; but the destruction of his armament will purchase you your province. Now in two days at most our troops will come, and then we will slay all the Free Companions."

"That is true," said Orestes, "and it is remarkable how you think of these things so quickly."

So Orestes was ruled by Ahasuerus, and Perion, through no merit of his own, departed unharmed.

Then Melicent was conducted to her own apartments; and eunuchs guarded her, while the battle was, and men she had not ever seen died by the score because her beauty was so great.

29.
How a Bargain Was Cried

NOW about sunset Melicent knelt in her oratory and laid all her grief before the Virgin, imploring counsel.

This place was in reality a chapel, which Demetrios had builded for Melicent in exquisite enjoyment. To furnish it he had sacked towns she never heard of, and had rifled two cathedrals, because the notion that the wife of Demetrios should own a Christian chapel appeared to him amusing. The Virgin, a masterpiece of Pietro di Vicenza, Demetrios had purchased by the interception of a free city's navy. It was a painted statue, very handsome.

The sunlight shone on Melicent through a richly coloured window wherein were shown the sufferings of Christ and the two thieves. This siftage made about her a welter of glowing and intermingling colours, above which her head shone with a clear halo.

This much Ahasuerus noted. He said:

"You offer tears to Miriam of Nazara. Yonder they are sacrificing a bull to Mithras. But I do not make either offering or prayer to any god. Yet of all persons in Nacumera I alone am sure of this day's outcome." Thus spoke the Jew Ahasuerus.

The woman stood erect now. She asked, "What of the day, Ahasuerus?"

"It has been much like other days that I have seen. The sun rose without any perturbation. And now it sinks as usual. Oh, true, there has been fighting. The sky has been clouded with arrows, and horses, nicer than their masters, have screamed because these soulless beasts were appalled by so much blood. Many women have become widows, and divers children are made orphans, because of two huge eyes they never saw. Puf! it is an old tale."

She said, "Is Perion hurt?"

"Is the dog hurt that has driven a cat into a tree? Such I estimate to be the position of Orestes and Perion. Ah, no, this Perion who was my captain once is as yet a lord without any peer in the fields where men contend in battle. But love has thrust him into a bag's end, and his fate is certain."

She spoke her steadfast resolution. "And my fate, too. For when Perion is trapped and slain I mean to kill myself."

"I am aware of that," he said. "Oh, women have these notions! Yet when the hour came, I think, you would not dare. For I know your beliefs concerning hell's geography, and which particular gulf of hell is reserved for all self-murderers."

Then Melicent waited for a while. She spoke later without any apparent emotion. "And how should I fear hell who crave a bitterer fate! Listen, Ahasuerus! I know that you desire me as a plaything very greatly. The infamy in which you wade attests as much. Yet you have schemed to no purpose if Perion dies, because the ways of death are always open. I would die many times rather than endure the touch of your finger. Ahasuerus, I have not any words wherewith to tell you of my loathing—"

"Turn then to bargaining," he said, and seemed aware of all her thoughts.

"Oh, to a hideous bargain. Let Perion be warned of those troops that will to-morrow outflank him. Let him escape. There is yet time. Do this, dark hungry man, and I will live." She shuddered here. "Yes, I will live and be obedient in all things to you, my purchaser, until you shall have wearied of me, or, at the least, until God has remembered."

His careful eyes were narrowed. "You would bribe me as you once bribed Demetrios? And to the same purpose? I think that fate excels less in invention than in cruelty."

She bitterly said, "Heaven help me, and what other wares have I to vend!"

He answered:

"None. No woman has in this black age; and therefore comfort you, my girl."

She hurried on. "Therefore anew I offer Melicent, who was a princess once. I cry a price for red lips and bright eyes and a fair woman's tender body without any blemish. I have no longer youth and happiness and honour to afford you as your toys. These three have long been strangers to me. Oh, very long! Yet all I have I offer for one charitable deed. See now how near you are to victory. Think now how gloriously one honest act would show in you who have betrayed each overlord you ever served."

He said:

"I am suspicious of strange paths, I shrink from practising unfamiliar virtues. My plan is fixed. I think I shall not alter it."

"Ah, no, Ahasuerus! think instead how beautiful I am. There is no comelier animal in all this big lewd world. Indeed I cannot count how many men have died because I am a comely animal—" She smiled as one who is too tired to weep. "That, too, is an old tale. Now I abate in value, it appears, very lamentably. For I am purchasable now just by one honest deed, and there is none who will barter with me."

He returned:

"You forget that a freed Perion would always have a sonorous word or two to say in regard to your bargainings. Demetrios bargained, you may remember. Demetrios was a dread lord. It cost him daily warfare to retain you. Now I lack swords and castles—I who dare love you much as Demetrios did—and I would be able to retain neither Melicent nor tranquil existence for an unconscionable while. Ah, no! I bear my former general no grudge. I merely recognise that while Perion lives he will not ever leave pursuit of you. I would readily concede the potency of his spurs, even were there need to look on you a second time— It happens that there is no need! Meanwhile I am a quiet man, and I abhor dissension. For the rest,

I do not think that you will kill yourself, and so I think I shall not alter my fixed plan."

He left her, and Melicent prayed no more. To what end, she reflected, need she pray, when there was no hope for Perion?

30.
How Melicent Conquered

INTO Melicent's bedroom, about two o'clock in the morning, came Ahasuerus the Jew. She sat erect in bed and saw him cowering over a lamp which his long glistening fingers shielded, so that the lean face of the man floated upon a little golden pool in the darkness. She marvelled that this detestable countenance had not aged at all since her first sight of it.

He smoothly said:

"Now let us talk. I have loved you for some while, fair Melicent."

"You have desired me," she replied.

"Faith, I am but as all men, whatever their age. Why, what the devil! man may have Javeh's breath in him, but even Scripture proves that man was made of clay." The Jew now puffed out his jaws as if in recollection. *"You are a handsome piece of flesh,* I thought when I came to you at Bellegarde, telling of Perion's captivity. I thought no more than this, because in my time I have seen a greater number of handsome women than you would suppose. Thereafter, on account of an odd reason which I had, I served Demetrios willingly enough. This son of Miramon Lluagor was able to pay me well, in a curious coinage. So I arranged the bungling snare Demetrios proposed—too gross, I thought it, to trap any woman living. Ohé, and why should I not lay an open and frank springe for you? Who else was a king's bride-to-be, young, beautiful, and blessed with wealth and honour and every other comfort which the world affords?" Now the Jew made as if to fling away a robe from his gaunt person. "And you cast this, all this, aside as nothing. I saw it done."

"Ah, but I did it to save Perion," she wisely said.

"Unfathomable liar," he returned, "you boldly and unscrupulously bought of life the thing which you most earnestly desired. Nor Solomon nor Periander has won more. And thus I saw that which no other man has seen. I saw the shrewd and dauntless soul of Melicent. And so I loved you, and I laid my plan—"

She said, "You do not know of love—"

"Yet I have builded him a temple," the Jew considered. He continued, with that old abhorrent acquiescence: "Now, a temple is admirable, but it is not builded until many labourers have dug and toiled waist-deep in dirt. Here, too, such spatterment seemed necessary. So I played, in fine, I played a cunning music. The pride of Demetrios, the jealousy of Callistion, and the greed of Orestes—these were as so many stops of that flute on which I played a cunning deadly music. Who forbids it?"

She motioned him, "Go on." Now she was not afraid.

"Come then to the last note of my music! You offer to bargain, saying, *Save Perion and have my body as your chattel.* I answer *Click!* The turning of a key solves all. Accordingly I have betrayed the castle of Nacumera, I have this night admitted Perion and his broad-shouldered men. They are killing Orestes yonder in the Court of Stars even while I talk with you." Ahasuerus laughed noiselessly. "Such vanity does not become a Jew, but I needs must do the thing with some magnificence. Therefore I do not give Sire Perion only his life. I give him also victory and much throat-cutting and an impregnable rich castle. Have I not paid the price, fair Melicent? Have I not won God's masterpiece through a small wire, a purse, and a big key?"

She answered, "You have paid."

He said:

"You will hold to your bargain? Ah, you have but to cry aloud, and you are rid of me. For this is Perion's castle."

She said, "Christ help me! You have paid my price."

Now the Jew raised his two hands in very horrible mirth. Said he:

"Oh, I am almost tempted to praise Javeh, who created the invincible soul of Melicent. For you have conquered: you have gained, as always, and at whatever price, exactly that which you most desired, and you do not greatly care about anything else. So, because of a word said you would arise and follow me on my dark ways if I commanded it. You will not weight the dice, not even at this pinch, when it would be so easy! For Perion is safe; and nothing matters in comparison with that, and you will not break faith, not even with me. You are inexplicable, you are stupid, and you are resistless. Again I see my Melicent, who is not just a pair of purple eyes and so much lovely flesh."

His face was as she had not ever known it now, and very tender. Ahasuerus said:

"My way to victory is plain enough. And yet there is an obstacle. For my fancy is taken by the soul of Melicent, and not by that handsome piece of flesh which all men—even Perion, madame!—have loved so long with remarkable infatuation. Accordingly I had not ever designed that the edifice on which I laboured should be the stable of my lusts. Accordingly I played my cunning music—and accordingly I give you Perion. I that am Ahasuerus win for you all which righteousness and honour could not win. At the last it is I who give you Perion, and it is I who bring you to his embrace. He must still be about his magnanimous butchery, I think, in the Court of Stars."

Ahasuerus knelt, kissing her hand.

"Fair Melicent, such abominable persons as Demetrios and I are fatally alike. We may deny, deride, deplore, or even hate, the sanctity of any noble lady accordingly as we elect; but there is for us no possible escape from worshipping it. Your wind-fed Perions, who will not ever acknowledge what sort of world we live in, are less quick to recognise the soul of Melicent. Such is our sorry consolation. Oh, you do not believe me yet. You will believe in the oncoming years. Meanwhile, O all-enduring and all-conquering! go now to your last labour; and —if my Brother dare concede as much—do you now conquer Perion."

Then he vanished. She never saw him any more.

She lifted the Jew's lamp. She bore it through the Women's Garden, wherein were many discomfortable shadows and no living being. She came to its outer entrance. Men were fighting there. She skirted a hideous conflict, and descended the Queen's Stairway, which led (as you have heard) toward the balcony about the Court of Stars. She found this balcony vacant.

Below her men were fighting. To the farther end of the court Orestes sprawled upon the red and yellow slabs—which now for the most part were red—and above him towered Perion of the Forest. The conqueror had paused to cleanse his sword upon the same divan Demetrios had occupied when Melicent first saw the proconsul; and as Perion turned, in the act of sheathing his sword, he perceived the dear familiar denizen of all his dreams. A tiny lamp glowed in her hand quite steadily.

"O Melicent," said Perion, with a great voice, "my task is done. Come now to me."

She instantly obeyed whose only joy was to please Perion. Descending the enclosed stairway, she thought how like its gloom was to the temporal unhappiness she had passed through in serving Perion.

He stood a dripping statue, for he had fought horribly. She came to him, picking her way among the slain. He trembled who was fresh from slaying. A flood of torchlight surged and swirled about them, and within a stone's cast Perion's men were despatching the wounded.

These two stood face to face and did not speak at all.

I think that he knew disappointment first. He looked to find the girl whom he had left on Fomor Beach.

He found a woman, the possessor still of a compelling beauty. Oh, yes, past doubt: but this woman was a stranger to him, as he now knew with an odd sense of sickness. Thus, then, had ended the quest of Melicent. Their love had flouted Time and Fate. These had revenged this insolence, it seemed to Perion, by an ironical conversion of each rebel into another person. For this was not the girl whom Perion had loved in far red-roofed Poictesme; this was not the girl for whom Perion had fought ten minutes since: and he—as Perion for the first time perceived—was not and never could be any more the Perion that girl had bidden return to her. It were as easy to evoke the Perion who had loved Mélusine. . . .

Then Perion perceived that love may be a power so august as to bedwarf consideration of the man and woman whom it sways. He saw that this is reasonable. I cannot justify this knowledge. I cannot even tell you just what great secret it was of which Perion became aware. Many men have seen the sunrise, but the serenity and awe and sweetness of this daily miracle, the huge assurance which it emanates that the beholder is both impotent and greatly beloved, is not entirely an affair of the sky's tincture. And thus it was with Perion. He knew what he could not explain. He knew such joy and terror as none has ever worded. A curtain had lifted briefly; and the familiar world which Perion knew about had appeared, for that brief instant, to be a painting upon that curtain.

Now, dazzled, he saw Melicent for the first time. . . .

I think he saw the lines already forming in her face, and knew that, but for him, this woman, naked now of gear and friends, had been to-night a queen among her own acclaiming people. I think he worshipped where he did not dare to love, as every man cannot but do when starkly fronted by the divine and stupendous unreason of a woman's choice, among so many other men, of him. And yet, I think that Perion recalled what Ayrart de Montors had said of women and their love, so long ago:—"They are more wise than we; and always they make us better by indomitably believing we are better than in reality a man can ever be."

I think that Perion knew, now, de Montors had been in the right. The pity and mystery and beauty of that world wherein High God had—scornfully?—placed a smug Perion, seemed to the Comte de la Forêt, I think, unbearable. I think a new and finer love smote Perion as a sword strikes.

I think he did not speak because there was no scope for words. I know that he knelt (incurious for once of victory) before this stranger who was not the Melicent whom he had sought so long, and that all consideration of a lost young Melicent departed from him, as mists leave our world when the sun rises.

I think that this was her high hour of triumph.

CÆTERA DESUNT

THE AFTERWORD

These lives made out of loves that long since were
Lives wrought as ours of earth and burning air,
Was such not theirs, the twain I take, and give
Out of my life to make their dead life live
Some days of mine, and blow my living breath
Between dead lips forgotten even of death?
So many and many of old have given my twain
Love and live song and honey-hearted pain.

THE AFTERWORD

THUS, rather suddenly, ends our knowledge of the love-business between Perion and Melicent. For at this point, as abruptly as it began, the one existing chronicle of their adventures makes conclusion, like a bit of interrupted music, and thereby affords conjecture no inconsiderable bounds wherein to exercise itself. Yet, in view of the fact that deductions as to what befell these lovers afterward can at best result in free-handed theorising, it seems more profitable in this place to speak very briefly of the fragmentary *Roman de Lusignan,* since the history of Melicent and Perion as set forth in this book makes no pretensions to be more than a rendering into English of this manuscript, with slight additions from the earliest known printed version of 1546.

2

M. Verville, in his monograph on Nicolas de

Caen,[1] considers it probable that the *Roman de Lusignan* was printed in Bruges by Colard Mansion at about the same time Mansion published the *Dizain des Reines.* This is possible; but until a copy of the book is discovered, our sole authority for the romance must continue to be the fragmentary MS. No. 503 in the Allonbian Collection.

Among the innumerable manuscripts in the British Museum there is perhaps none which opens a wider field for guesswork. In its entirety the *Roman de Lusignan* was, if appearances are to be trusted, a leisured and ambitious handling of the Melusina legend; but in the preserved portion Melusina figures hardly at all. We have merely the final chapters of what would seem to have been the first half, or perhaps the first third, of the complete narrative; so that this manuscript account of Melusina's beguilements breaks off, fantastically, at a period by many years anterior to a date which those better known versions of Jean d'Arras and Thuring von Ringoltingen select as the only appropriate starting-point.

By means of a few elisions, however, the episodic story of Melicent and of the men who loved

[1] Paul Verville, *Notice sur la vie de Nicolas de Caen,* p. 112 (Rouen, 1911).

Melicent has been disembedded from what survives of the main narrative. This episode may reasonably be considered as complete in itself, in spite of its precipitous commencement; we are not told anything very definite concerning Perion's earlier relations with Melusina, it is true, but then they are hardly of any especial importance. And speculations as to the tale's perplexing chronology, or as to the curious treatment of the Ahasuerus legend, wherein Nicolas so strikingly differs from his precursors, Matthew Paris and Philippe Mouskes, or as to the probable course of latter incidents in the romance (which must almost inevitably have reached its climax in the foundation of the house of Lusignan by Perion's son Raymondin and Melusina) are more profitably left to M. Verville's ingenuity.

3

One feature, though, of this romance demands particular comment. The happenings of the Melicent-episode pivot remarkably upon *domnei*—upon chivalric love, upon the *Frowendienst* of the minnesingers, or upon "woman-worship," as we might bunglingly translate a word for which in English there is no precisely equivalent synonym. Therefore this English version of the Melicent-episode has been called *Domnei,* at whatever price of unintelligibility.

For there is really no other word or combination of words which seems quite to sum up, or even indicate this precise attitude toward life. *Domnei* was less a preference for one especial woman than a code of philosophy. "The complication of opinions and ideas, of affections and habits," writes Charles Claude Fauriel,[1] "which prompted the chevalier to devote himself to the service of a lady, and by which he strove to prove to her his love and to merit hers in return, was expressed by the single word *domnei.*"

And this, of course, is true enough. Yet *domnei* was even more than a complication of opinions and affections and habits: it was also a malady and a religion quite incommunicably blended.

Thus you will find that Dante—to cite only the most readily accessible of mediæval amorists—enlarges as to *domnei* in both these last-named aspects impartially. *Domnei* suspends all his senses save that of sight, makes him turn pale, causes tremors in his left side, and sends him to bed "like a little beaten child, in tears"; throughout you have the manifestations of *domnei* described in terms befit-

[1] *Histoire de la littérature provençale,* p. 330 (Adler's translation, New York, 1860).

ting the symptoms of a physical disease: but as concerns the other aspect, Dante never wearies of reiterating that it is *domnei* which has turned his thoughts toward God; and with terrible sincerity he beholds in Beatricè de' Bardi the highest illumination which Divine Grace may permit to humankind. "This is no woman; rather it is one of heaven's most radiant angels," he says with terrible sincerity.

With terrible sincerity, let it be repeated: for the service of *domnei* was never, as some would affect to interpret it, a modish and ordered affectation; the histories of Peire de Maënzac, of Guillaume de Caibestaing, of Geoffrey Rudel, of Ulrich von Liechtenstein, of the Monk of Pucibot, of Pons de Capdueilh, and even of Peire Vidal and Guillaume de Balaun, survive to prove it was a serious thing, a stark and life-disposing reality. *En cor gentil domnei per mort no passa,* as Nicolas himself declares. The service of *domnei* involved, it in fact invited, anguish; it was a martyrdom whereby the lover was uplifted to saintship and the lady to little less than, if anything less than, godhead.

For it was a canon of *domnei,* it was the very essence of *domnei,* that the woman one loves is providentially set between her lover's apprehension and God, as the mobile and vital image and corporeal reminder of heaven, as a quick symbol of beauty and holiness, of purity and perfection. In her the lover views—embodied, apparent to human sense, and even accessible to human enterprise—all qualities of God which can be comprehended by merely human faculties. It is precisely as such an intermediary that Melicent figures toward Perion, and, in a somewhat different degree, toward Ahasuerus—since Ahasuerus is of necessity apart in all things from the run of humanity.

Yet instances were not lacking in the service of *domnei* where worship of the symbol developed into a religion sufficing in itself, and became competitor with worship of what the symbol primarily represented—such instances as have their analogues in the legend of Ritter Tannhäuser, or in Aucassin's resolve in the romance to go down into hell with "his sweet mistress whom he so much loves," or (here perhaps most perfectly exampled) in Arnaud de Merveil's naïve declaration that whatever portion of his heart belongs to God heaven holds in vassalage to Adelaide de Beziers. It is upon this darker and rebellious side of *domnei,* of a religion pathetically dragged dustward by the luxuriance and efflorescence of over-passionate service, that Nicolas has touched in depicting Demetrios.

4

Nicolas de Caen, himself the servitor *par amours* of Isabella of Burgundy, has elsewhere written of *domnei* (in his *Le Roi Amaury*) in terms such as it may not be entirely out of place to transcribe here. Baalzebub, as you may remember, has been discomfited in his endeavours to ensnare King Amaury and is withdrawing in disgust.

"A pest upon this *domnei!*"[1] the fiend growls. "Nay, the match is at an end, and I may speak in perfect candour now. I swear to you that, given a man clear-eyed enough to see that a woman by ordinary is nourished much as he is nourished, and is subjected to every bodily infirmity which he endures and frets beneath, I do not often bungle matters. But when a fool begins to flounder about the world, dead-drunk with adoration of an immaculate woman—a monster which, as even the man's own judgment assures him, does not exist and never will exist—why, he becomes as unman-

[1] Quoted with minor alterations from Watson's version.

ageable as any other maniac when a frenzy is upon him. For then the idiot hungers after a life so high-pitched that his gross faculties may not so much as glimpse it; he is so rapt with impossible dreams that he becomes oblivious to the nudgings of his most petted vice; and he abhors his own innate and perfectly natural inclination to cowardice, and filth, and self-deception. He, in fine, affords me and all other rational people no available handle; and, in consequence, he very often flounders beyond the reach of my whisperings. There may be other persons who can inform you why such blatant folly should thus be the master-word of evil, but for my own part, I confess to ignorance."

"Nay, that folly, as you term it, and as hell will always term it, is alike the riddle and the master-word of the universe," the old king replies. . . .

And Nicolas whole-heartedly believed that this was true. We do not believe this, quite, but it may be that we are none the happier for our dubiety.

EXPLICIT

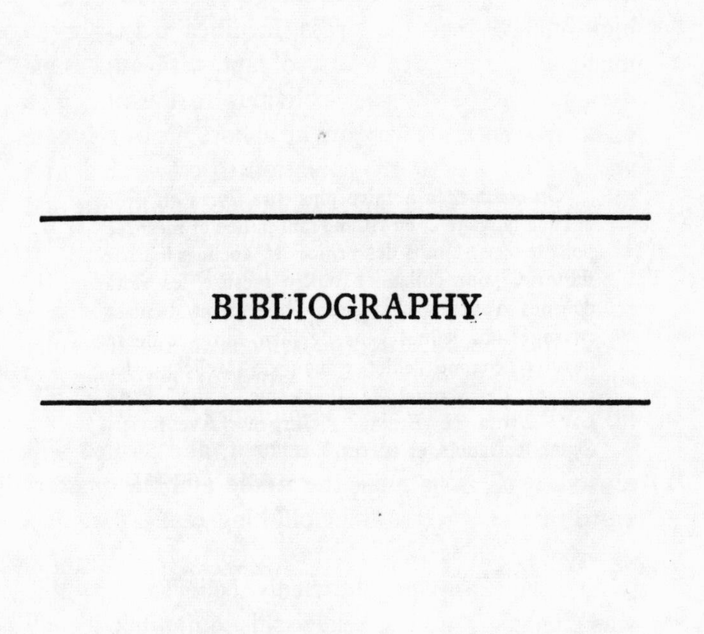

BIBLIOGRAPHY

"On commença à faire plusieurs livres en gros et rude langage et en rithme mal taillée et mesurée pour le passe-temps des princes et aucunes fois par flatterie, pour collauder oultre mesure les faits d'armes d'aucuns chevaliers, à ce qu'on donnast courage aux jeunes gens de bien faire et de se hardier, comme ledict roman de Melicent, les romans de Manuel de Poictesme, Lancelot du Lac, Artus de Bretagne, Iurgen l'Aventurier, Ogier le Danois, et autres."

—Jehan Bouclet.

BIBLIOGRAPHY

I. Les Amants de Melicent, Traduction moderne, annotée et procedée d'un notice historique sur Nicolas de Caen, par l'Abbé * * * A Paris. Pour Iaques Keruer aux deux Cochetz, Rue S. Iaques, M. D. XLVI. Avec Privilege du Roy. The somewhat abridged reprint of 1788 was believed to be the first version printed in French, until the discovery of this unique volume in 1917.

II. Armageddon; or the Great Day of the Lord's Judgement: a Parœnesis to Prince Henry—Melicent; an heroicke poeme intended, drawne from French bookes, the First Booke, by Sir William Allonby. London. Printed for Nathaniel Butler, dwelling at the *Pied Bull,* at Saint Austen's Gate. 1626.

III. Perion und Melicent, zum erstenmale aus dem Französischen ins Deutsche übersetzt, von J. H. G. Löwe. Stuttgart und Tübingen, 1823.

IV. Los Negociantes do Don Perion, publicado por Plancher-Seignot. Rio de Janiero,

1827. The translator's name is not given. The preface is signed R. L.

V. La donna di Demetrio, Historia piacevole e morale, da Antonio Checino. Milan, 1833.

VI. Prindsesses Melicent, oversat af Le Roman de Lusignan, og udgivna paa Dansk vid R. Knös. Copenhagen, 1840.

VII. Antiquæ Fabulæ et Comediæ, edid. G. Rask. Göttingen, 1852. Vol. II, p. 61 *et seq*. "De Fide Melicentis"—an abridged version of the romance.

VIII. Perion en Melicent, voor de Nederlandsche Jeugduiitgegeven door J. M. L. Wolters. Groningen, 1862.

IX. Nouvelles Françoises en prose du XIVe et de XVe siècle, Les textes anciens, edités et annotés par MM. Armin et Moland. Lyons, 1880. Vol. IV, p. 89 *et seq.*, "Le Roman de la Belle Melicent"—a much condensed form of the story.

X. The Soul of Melicent, by James Branch Cabell. Illustrated in colour by Howard Pyle. New York, 1913. This rendering was made, of course, before the discovery of the 1546 version, and so had not the benefit of that volume's interesting variants from the abridgment of 1788.

XI. Cinq Ballades de Nicolas de Caen, traduites en verse du Roman de Lusignan, par Mme. Adolphe Galland, et mises en musique par Raoul Bidoche. Paris, 1898.

XII. Le Liure de Mélusine en frācoys, par Jean d'Arras. Geneva, 1478.

XIII. Historia de la linda Melosyna. Tolosa, 1489.

XIV. Een san sonderlingke schone ende wonderlike historie, die men warachtich kout te syne ende autentick sprekende van eenre vrouwen gheheeten Melusine. Tantwerpen, 1500.

XV. Die Histori oder Geschicht von der edle und schönen Melusina. Augsburg, 1547.

XVI. L'histoire de Mélusine, fille du roy d'Albanie et de dame Pressine, revue et mise en meilleur langage que par cy devant. Lyons, 1597.

XVII. Le roman de Mélusine, princesse de Lusignan, avec l'histoire de Geoffry, surnommé à la Grand Dent, par Nodot. Paris, 1700.

XVIII. Kronyke Kratochwilne, o ctné a slech netné Panně Meluzijně. Prag, 1760.

XIX. Wunderbare Geschichte von der edeln und schönen Melusina, welche eine

Tochter des König Helmus und ein Meerwunder gewesen ist. Nurnberg, without date: reprinted in Marbach's VOLKSBÜCHER, Leipzig, 1838.

XX. MELLUSINE, poème relatif à cette fée poitevine, composé dans le XIVe siècle par Couldrette, publié pour la première fois d'après les manuscrits de la bibliothèque impériale par Francisque Michel. Niort, Robin et L. Favre, 1854. This is the first, and I believe the only, printed version of the older *Roman de Lusignan,* which was completed in 1401, and exists in a number of variant manuscripts.